# SUNDAY THE RABBI STAYED HOME

Also Available in Large Print
by Harry Kemelman

*Tuesday the Rabbi Saw Red*
*Wednesday the Rabbi Got Wet*

# SUNDAY
# THE RABBI
# STAYED
# HOME

## Harry Kemelman

G.K.HALL&CO.

 Boston, Massachusetts

1977

**Library of Congress Cataloging in Publication Data**

Kemelman, Harry.
  Sunday the rabbi stayed home.

  Large print ed.
  1.  Large type books.  I.  Title.
[PZ4.K3184Su  1977]  [PS3561.E398]  813'.5'4  77-21552
ISBN 0-8161-6499-1

Published in Large Print by arrangement with G. P. Putnam's Sons

Set in Compugraphic 18 pt English Times

*To my children —*
*Ruth and George,*
*Arthur,*
*Diane and Stanley*

# 1

"Now, that's what I call praying, Rabbi," said Harvey Andelman. "We finished five minutes" — a glance at his watch — "no, seven minutes ahead of schedule."

The rabbi, Rabbi David Small, smiled as he continued to roll up his phylacteries. He was young, in his mid-thirties; although in good health, he was pale and thin and carried his head slightly forward, as though peering nearsightedly at a book. He had indeed gone through the service at breakneck speed and felt a little sheepish about it. "You see, I'm going on a trip —"

"Sure, and you want to make an early start — naturally." It seemed perfectly reasonable to Andelman, who had a market in Salem and was always trying to speed up the morning prayers so that he could get to his place of business in good time. He was in torment on those days when they had to wait around to secure the ten men needed for the minyan; and as soon as he spotted the tenth man, he would wave him on as he might a runner nearing the tape, calling, "C'mon, c'mon, let's get going." But now, luxuriating in his unexpected five, no, seven minutes of grace, he waited for the rabbi to put away his phylacteries and prayer shawl. "When Wasserman leads, or the cantor, you'd think it was Yom Kippur, that they got all day. And come to think of it, I guess they have. But the rest of us, we got jobs and businesses to go to. Well, be seeing you, Rabbi," he said, loping off to his car.

Because he felt guilty about having hurried the prayers, Rabbi Small slowed down his pace to a stroll as he went along the corridor that lead to his study. For the first time in a long while he noted the bare white cinder-block outer wall divided halfway up to no purpose by a strip of black plastic; the similarly divided yellow-glazed brick inner wall; the rubber tile floor, gleaming from a recent waxing, on which only the circled imprint of the floor polisher gave some semblance of design. It had the sterile feel of a hospital corridor.

When he had first come to Barnard's Crossing six years ago, the temple had been brand-spanking-new, and its modernity had a gay sparkle. But now it was beginning to show signs of age. There were scuff marks along the wall, and at one point near the ceiling there was a yellow stain where a pipe joint had let go. The rabbi could not help feeling that the older temples, with their carved paneling in mahogany or walnut, tended to age more gracefully.

As he neared his study he heard his phone ringing and hurried to answer it. He assumed it was Miriam with a last-minute request to pick up something — a bottle of milk, some rolls — at the grocery, but it was a man's voice, the tone accusing.

"Rabbi? Ben Gorfinkle. I called your house, and your wife said you were at the temple."

"The morning services —"

"Of course," said the temple president,

3

as though conceding it was a legitimate excuse. "You know, Rabbi, the damnedest thing happened this morning. We were chewing the fat over a second cup of coffee, and Sarah mentioned that you were going to Binkerton."

"I told you several weeks ago that I was going," the rabbi remarked.

"Oh, I knew you were going to hold Sabbath services for some Hillel group, but I didn't realize you were going to Mass State at Binkerton. It just goes to show you what a small world it is. My Stuart is there."

"Oh, really? I didn't know that."

"Look, I thought maybe you'd say hello for us and —"

"But of course, Mr. Gorfinkle."

"I'm sure he'll come to your service, but just in case he gets tied up, maybe if you took his phone number —"

"Of course. Just a minute — let me get a piece of paper." He jotted down the number.

"It's a dormitory, so if he's not there, you can leave a message."

"I understand."

"If you call him when you get in, maybe he could show you around the campus."

"That's an idea." He was aware of a voice in the background, and Gorfinkle said, "Just a minute, Rabbi." Then after an interval of muffled sounds through the covered receiver, "Of course, he may have a class in the afternoon or have some studying to do."

The rabbi smiled to himself. Mrs. Gorfinkle must have pointed out that their son might not like the idea of being saddled with the rabbi and his family for the afternoon. "That's all right. We'll probably be pretty tired after our trip and will want to rest up."

"Well, it's a thought, anyway. When are you coming back, Rabbi?"

"Saturday night, right after Havdalah."

"Really?" Gorfinkle sounded surprised. "I thought Stuart said —" He sounded his hearty self again. "Well, anyway, it just occurred to me —"

"Yes?" The rabbi felt sure that he was now to hear the real reason for the call.

"If you've got room in your car, if it's

5

not crowding you or inconveniencing you in any way — you see, Stuart will be coming home for Passover, and they've got a week's vacation —"

"That I could give him a lift back?"

"Only if it wouldn't be any trouble to you."

"I'd be very happy to, Mr. Gorfinkle."

He had no sooner hung up when there was a rap on the door, and without waiting to be invited, in came Morton Brooks, the principal of the religious school. He was a bouncy, youngish man of forty, with a kind of theatrical flamboyance about him.

"Thank God I caught you before you left. When I got the call, I came right over."

"What happened?"

"Arlene Feldberg broke out with measles! The doctor was over last night, but Mrs. Feldberg didn't think to notify me until this morning." He sounded betrayed.

"Arlene Feldberg?"

Brooks nervously fingered the long strands of hair that he had carefully combed to cover an incipient bald spot. "You know Arlene Feldberg, the little girl from the first grade who's supposed to say the Four Questions in English at the seder."

"Oh, Harry Feldberg's child. Well, that's all right." The rabbi was considerably relieved. For a moment he had thought the principal was concerned about a possible epidemic. "The Haggadahs we're using have the English translation on the opposite page. Or I suppose the little boy — what's his name?"

"Geoffrey Blumenthal."

"I'm sure Geoffrey can give the translation after he reads it in the Hebrew."

"Impossible, Rabbi."

"You mean he doesn't know what the Hebrew means?"

"Of course he knows," said Brooks indignantly, "but there's a big difference between reading and being able to recite it without adequate rehearsal. But even if there were time to coach him properly, it's still impossible. In fact, it would be adding insult to injury to let him have both parts. The Feldbergs would never forgive me, and they'd talk about it to their friends, and they include the Paffs and the Edelsteins. I assure you, Rabbi, we'd never hear the end of it."

"I see. And Geoffrey is a —"

"Blumenthal, of course — friends of the Gorfinkles, the Epsteins, and the Brennermans. They're cousins of the Brennermans, in fact."

"Oh, come, Morton. Isn't that rather silly?"

"Not at all," said the principal gravely. "Believe me, Rabbi, this is my third school, and I know how these things work. If you don't mind my saying so, I think you would be wise to pay a little more attention to the politics in the congregation. Oh, you attend the board meetings regularly, but the important developments take place in the school. That's where it really shows up."

"In the religious school?" The rabbi made no attempt to hide his amusement.

"Of course. The High Holidays are once a year. And the lesser holidays, if

8

they fall during the middle of the week, we don't get more than seventy-five attending services, like on Friday nights. But the school — the kids go three times a week, and they report anything that happens the minute they get home. You know how we Jews feel about our kids. Any little slight or fancied unfairness, you'd think from the way the parents carry on it was a pogrom."

The rabbi smiled. "So what do you want to do about the present — er, crisis?"

"Well, it's a problem. Most of the members, as you know, hold their own seders at home, so we don't have too many children from the first grade who are coming to the temple seder. And the Paff group, who tend to be a little older, have fewer children in the first grade, anyway. But they have better representation in the upper grades. So I thought about that bit about the four kinds of sons. You know, the wise, the foolish, the simple, the wicked son."

"I know," said the rabbi dryly.

"Yes, of course, Rabbi. Well, I was

thinking how would it be if we could act it out, see. You'd say the introductory paragraph, and then the lights would go dark, and we'd have a spotlight focused right in front on the head table.'' With tiny steps, he approached the rabbi's desk, his hands moving to outline the cone of light from the spot. ''Then we could have the sons come on one at a time, see. The wise son, say, might come in wearing glasses and reading a book or maybe fiddling with a slide rule. Then he'd suddenly look up and ask his question. Only, the way I see it, we'd modernize it and have him say something like, 'Golly, this is groovy, Dad. How come the Lord our God asked us to do all these things?' And the way I visualized the wicked son, he'd be dressed in a black leather jacket and one of those peaked caps and sun goggles, or maybe we could have him dressed as a hippie — you know, barefoot with beads and long hair and faded blue jeans.'' He slouched, his head lolling to one side, and he spoke out of one side of his mouth, as though there were a cigarette dangling there. '' 'Hey, how

10

come you cats snazzied up your pad like this? Crazy, man, crazy.' Do you get the idea?''

''And how would this help your particular situation?''

''Well, we have a wider choice among the older children. I had the Edelstein boy tabbed for the part of the wicked son. And being all dressed up, the only one in costume, you might say, it would go a long way —''

''Have you thought of a rock and roll band for the chants?''

Brooks looked at him. ''Now there's an idea, Rabbi.''

''No, Morton. No,'' he said firmly. ''We'll stick to a traditional seder if you don't mind. And let the Blumenthals and Feldbergs just make the best of it.'' He rose and edged to the door. ''I really have to run now.''

''Well, think about it over the weekend, won't you, Rabbi?'' Brooks pleaded.

''I'll give it all my free time,'' said the rabbi with unwonted sarcasm.

But Brooks was not to be put off. ''No, seriously, Rabbi, what's wrong with livening up the ceremony so's to capture the interest of the kids? Everybody's doing it now — the Catholics, everybody. They've even held jazz masses. After all, the seder's a celebration. Why shouldn't they have a good time?"

The rabbi stopped at the door. "Because, Morton, the Passover seder is something more than a celebration. It's a ritual in which every step is spelled out — and for a purpose. The whole point of a ritual is that it should be repeated exactly every time it is performed for it to have the proper effect. And now if you don't mind, I really am in something of a hurry."

Outside, he stopped for a moment to make sure the windows of his study were closed in case it should rain over the weekend. The exterior of the building was also showing signs of wear, he saw. The stainless steel columns, which Christian Sorensen, the architect, had said were intended to suggest "the purity of the religion and its resistance to the decay and erosion of time," had taken on a dull yellowish tinge — the effect of the salt air, no doubt. And the long walls of glazed white brick that jutted out from either side of the tall boxlike building and sloped away in gentle curves — "like a pair of open and embracing arms calling on people to come and worship" — were chipped here and there and showed black spaces like missing teeth.

In the parking lot the rabbi was delayed once again. Mr. Wasserman, the first president of the congregation, hailed him as he was getting into his car. Wasserman, now in his seventies, was thin and frail after his recent illness, and the hand he put on the rabbi's arm showed blue veins through transparent skin. He spoke softly, his speech not so much accented as showing special care to be correct.

"You'll be back for the board meeting Sunday, won't you, Rabbi?"

"Oh, certainly. We're planning to start back Saturday right after Havdalah, say six o'clock, and we should be home by nine — ten at the latest."

"That's good."

The rabbi paused in the act of getting in behind the wheel. "Are you expecting

13

something important to come up at the meeting?"

"Expecting? I'm always expecting, almost any day, but especially on Sundays when the board meets. This Sunday it could be something serious."

"Why this Sunday?"

Wasserman held up a finger. "Because next Sunday is the first seder, so there won't be a meeting." He held up a second finger. "The next Sunday is again the holiday, so again won't be a meeting. So if Gorfinkle is planning something serious, this Sunday would be a good day, because there wouldn't be another meeting for three weeks." He held up three fingers.

"And if he decides to do something serious, as you put it, how could I stop it?"

"You're the rabbi. That means you're not on one side or the other. You're like neutral, so you can say things that the rest of us can't."

"You're thinking of the committee changes that the president will make?" He settled into the car. "He'll make them sooner or later, anyway."

Wasserman shook his head. "But it will cause trouble, and better later than sooner. You're a rabbi, but I'm an old man. A lot that I've seen, maybe you only know from reading about it. It's like in a marriage. If an open break doesn't develop, it can be cured. After all, there are couples who quarrel almost from the day they get married. If one of them doesn't pack up and move out and go see a lawyer yet, there's a good chance the marriage will last."

"Isn't that being a little —" He looked at the old man; he was obviously troubled, so he changed his tack. "After all, Mr. Wasserman, it's only a board meeting."

Mr. Wasserman looked at him steadily. "Try to be there, Rabbi."

As he drove home to pick up Miriam and Jonathan, he found himself resenting the role he was expected to play. He was a rabbi — by tradition a scholar and teacher; why should he be mixed up with matters of faction and politics? Even Jacob Wasserman, whom he respected and regarded as one of his few real friends in the Jewish community — the one man

15

who should have an understanding of the traditional role of the rabbi — even he was involving him in the tawdry politics of the temple. It was almost as though they resented his taking a couple of days off.

It had all started a month ago when Rabbi Robert Dorfman, Hillel director and religious advisor to the Jewish students of Mass State, Western Division, at Binkerton, and his wife, Nancy, had driven east to visit her folks in Lynn. They had dropped in on the Smalls in Barnard's Crossing, because it was close by and the two men had been at the seminary together. In the course of conversation Bob Dorfman mentioned that he had applied for a pulpit in New Jersey.

"They've invited me to come down and conduct Friday and Saturday services."

"Sounds encouraging."

"It is, but I wish they had chosen some other date. That's the weekend before our spring vacation."

"And the Hillel people won't let you off for that weekend?" Rabbi Small sounded surprised.

"Oh, there's no trouble that way. It's

just that with the Passover coming during the vacation, I feel that I ought to conduct that going-away service."

"Why not ask the New Jersey people for a postponement or an alternate date?"

Rabbi Dorfman shook his head. "You know how it is. They may be having a bunch of candidates for a whole series of Sabbaths."

"You're pretty keen on this?"

"Oh, yes," said Dorfman. "Hillel work is all right, and working with college kids is important, but I'd like to get a regular congregation." He laughed self-consciously. "I'd like to make a speech of benediction at a Bar Mitzvah once in a while. I suppose it's the messianic delusion that we all suffer from a little or we wouldn't get into this business in the first place, but I have the feeling that what I can say at that time might strike the youngster just right. I'd like to be present at a *brith* —"

"And give a eulogy at a grave?"

"Yes, even that, if it could give comfort to the family." Bob Dorfman was stout and round-faced, and as he looked eagerly at his friend he seemed much younger, like a rosy-cheeked schoolboy hoping for his teacher's approval.

"Believe me," said Rabbi Small, "like most things, it doesn't come up to expectation. In a Hillel job, on the other hand, you have lots of time to yourself; you're in an academic atmosphere; you can study."

"But you're not involved in the real world."

"Maybe you're lucky. At least with a Hillel job you get security. In a congregation — in this real world of yours — you never can tell when you're going to step on the toes of somebody important and find you don't have a job."

The other grinned. "I know. I've heard that you've had your troubles, but that's all past, and you're all set now. You're on a long-term contract —"

Rabbi Small shook his head slowly. "Our contracts are service contracts, which means that legally — that is, as something you can sue for in a court of law — they're about useless. Even if you could, if you did sue, you'd merely insure

18

your never getting another pulpit. As you know, I was given a five-year contract, and when it expires at the end of this year, I suppose I will be offered another, probably at an increase in salary."

"So," said Dorfman, "you're all set."

"There are other drawbacks, though. For one thing, it's a full-time job. You're involved with the congregation twenty-four hours a day. Your time is not your own." He smiled. "You might find it a little wearing, even if it did give you a chance to officiate at a *brith* or a Bar Mitzvah."

"Oh, it's not only that," said Dorfman. "It's not only that I want to get into congregational work; I also want to get out of Hillel work. There's the matter of money; with a growing family, I've got to think of the future. But also I don't feel effective with these college kids. They're the wrong age for me. I don't feel that I'm getting across to them. They know everything, and they're cynical about it."

"Sometimes they're affected more than they show," said David Small. "I don't get to see too many of them, of course, only those who come under my hands here in Barnard's Crossing — kids I've had in post-confirmation classes. They usually drop in on me when they're home on vacation. To me they seem keen and vital. When they're cynical, it's because they're basically idealistic and they've been disappointed."

"Yes, but if kids were all you saw —"

"I suppose. Look, would it help if I came down to sub for you that weekend?"

Dorfman's face lit up. "Gosh, David, that would be wonderful." Then immediately it clouded. "But could you arrange it at your end?"

"I don't see why not. The Brotherhood conducts one service each year. This year I think it's the week before the one you're interested in. I'll check my calendar. But it shouldn't be too hard to change it to the following week, and I could then come down to Binkerton."

Miriam and Jonathan were all dressed and waiting for him when he drove up to the door. Tiny and vivacious-looking, Miriam had wide blue eyes, an open countenance, and a firm, determined little chin.

"Does he have to be bundled up like that?" her husband asked. "He'll roast."

"The weather is so changeable. I can always unzip his snowsuit if it gets too warm."

"All right. Get in. Let's get started."

Miriam started to close the door and then stopped as she heard the phone ring inside. "Just a second," she called out. "The phone."

"Don't answer it," he shouted.

She stopped. "Why not?"

"Because I want to get away. I'm tired."

She looked at him doubtfully and then closed the door, while inside the phone continued to ring.

Silently she strapped Jonathan into his harness in the front seat and then took her place beside him. As they drove off he repeated by way of apology, "I'm tired — just plain tired." and then, "I hurried through the prayers this morning, just saying the words, and I was short with Morton Brooks and annoyed with

21

Mr. Wasserman and —"

She patted his hand on the wheel. "That's all right, David. Everybody needs a little change once in a while."

# 2

The store was large as stores in Barnard's Crossing go, fully twenty feet wide and more than twice as deep. The windows were grimy and the display ledges behind them dusty. A long time ago they had been decorated with crepe paper, with flutings and rosettes and streamers of a poisonous green and saccharine pink — originally an elaborate Coca-Cola display. But the colors had faded and in places were badly water-spotted. The curvaceous cardboard models in one-piece bathing suits, probably quite daring at the time but now sadly old-fashioned, were still sitting, legs drawn up under them to emphasize the curve of the thigh, backs straight, and breasts firm and high with the suggestion of the nipple under the bathing suit, eyes half-closed, bottles of

Coca-Cola held to lips parted in anticipatory pleasure. Scattered around among the folds of crepe paper were dusty bottles of Coca-Cola, one of which had leaked open long ago, oozing its contents along the window ledge in a narrow, viscous streak.

Up against the window cases and blocking them off from easy access, which perhaps explained why the leaking Coke bottle had never been removed, were a cigarette vending machine, a jukebox, two pinball machines, and a steel tub of bottled soda embedded in crushed ice.

Along one wall was a large ornate marble soda fountain, behind which, lettered in black crayon across the flyspecked mirror, was a sign: FOUNTAIN OUT OF ORDER. Boxes of packaged cookies, doughnuts, and bags of peanuts were set on the marble counter top. On the opposite wall there were racks of magazines, paperback books, and greeting cards; and across the back of the store were shelves with notebooks, boxes of pencils, blocks of paper, boxes of rulers, erasers, compasses, pencil sharpeners, tubes of mucilage, rolls of tape, balls of twine, key rings, combs, hand mirrors, and other paraphernalia that school youngsters might want.

In the rear of the store was an old-fashioned rolltop desk and an antique swivel chair, its feet held together by several loops of baling wire, which also served as a footrest. In the center there were half a dozen round tables and chairs, where teen-agers would congregate.

The sign in front said: BOOKS AND STATIONERY, JOSEPH BEGG, ESQUIRE, PROP. Mr. Begg was a vigorous, muscular man of fifty, with a large bald head which was seldom seen, since he wore a hat all the time, who presided over his store from his rolltop desk in the rear. He was an unfriendly, crusty man, gruff and cantankerous, yet the store was a popular spot with the youngsters. They waited on themselves, picking up a package of cookies at the counter, a bottle of soda from the cooler, and then reported to the rear to show their purchases and pay up. They always called him Mr. Begg, although some of the older boys ventured

25

to call him Squire because of the sign outside. It was the nearest they ever came to joking with him. "Coke and doughnut. Twenty cents, Mr. Begg," they'd say and hand over money, which he tossed into an old cigar box on his desk. Or sometimes, "Change for the pinball machine, Mr. Begg, please," and he would examine the bill or coin suspiciously before grudgingly handing over the change. When they finished their drink, they were expected to put the empty bottle in the rack, and if they forgot, he called out sharply, "You there, put that bottle away," and they meekly complied.

Years ago Mr. Begg had taught at the high school and even had tenure, but he had left. No one, certainly none of his young patrons, knew why. He had served a term as selectman, but he no longer attended the annual town meetings and did not bother with town politics except to fire off an occasional letter of violent protest to the weekly newspaper — usually directed against some proposed plan to benefit the young, such as taking over land by eminent domain to

26

build a playground.

"He can't stand kids," was the usual explanation. "That's why he gave up teaching."

"But that place of his — only kids go there."

"Well, you know how it is: He started it as a bookstore, and then he added some greeting cards and some stationery items. Then when he found that mostly kids came, he put in other stuff for them. After all, the guy's got to make a living."

Friday morning Begg came in late. He had not been back at his desk more than a few minutes when the door opened and Moose Carter loafed in. "Hey, where you been, Squire?" He was a large muscular boy with the square shoulders and thick neck of a football player. He had blue eyes and a short, tilted nose and an eager grin. "I was down half an hour ago, and the place was shut tight." Begg did not deign to reply but turned to one side and spat in a cuspidor down by his left leg.

The young man did not take offense. "You going to be fixing up your place for the summer?"

"I'll be taking off the storm doors and windows and putting up the screens," the other admitted.

"Won't you be wanting some help?"

"I can use some," he said grudgingly. "Dollar and a half an hour."

"That's not much. I get two bucks an hour at the bowling alley and sometimes tips."

"I'm paying you a dollar and a half."

Moose shrugged. "Oh, all right. When do you want me?"

"Sunday morning, first thing."

A thought came to Moose. "Hey, Sunday — it ought to be more for Sunday."

"Why?" Beggs looked up humorlessly. "Because you'll miss going to church with your family?"

Moose laughed. "All right, I'll be there." He looked around and then dropped his voice. "Say, Squire, I got a date for tonight. How about some safes?"

"Three for a dollar."

"Look, I'm a little short right now. How about cuffing it against my pay for Sunday?"

Begg studied the face of the young man, then pulled open a desk drawer and reached inside. He handed Moose a small tin container. The young man slipped it into his trouser pocket. "Thanks, Squire." And then with a grin, "And my girl thanks you, too."

# 3

The key was under the mat. While the rabbi, hampered by a suitcase and an armful of coats, struggled with the lock, Miriam kept a tight hold on Jonathan, arms and legs spread like a starfish as he tried to make for the jungle gym he had spied in the backyard. "No, Jonathan, later," she said automatically. "You've got to have your lunch first and then your nap, and *then* you can go out and play."

They trooped into the reception hall and stood there for a moment, looking left and right at the dining room and facing living room. As Miriam stooped to extricate her young son from his snowsuit, the rabbi wandered into the living room toward a bookcase to inspect the titles. He selected a book and began to thumb through it. Then he sat down on the couch; and a moment later, his eyes still focused on the book, he had unlaced his shoes and kicked them off and stretched out on the couch, his head propped against the arm and the book held high to catch the light from the window.

Miriam found a coat hanger in the hall closet and hung up the snowsuit. She had put away the coats that her husband had left draped over the valise when she noticed the envelope on the hall table with her name printed across it in large block letters. She drew out a couple of sheets of paper typed single-space.

"Dear Miriam," she read aloud. "Welcome to Binkerton and Mass State, Western Division. I hope you followed instructions and didn't bring food. Everything is prepared — a complete Sabbath meal and enough for the weekend. It's all in the refrigerator, and all you have to do is heat it up. Pilot light doesn't work on left front burner. Use matches (in cupboard over stove) . . . Kiddush wine in dining room sideboard . . . meat dishes — blue edging — in cupboard on the right as you face kitchen windows . . . meat silver also on right — floral pattern . . . meat pots and pans in right cupboard . . . dairy utensils all on left . . . when washing dishes, watch out for kitchen faucet — squirts sideways when turned on full . . . arranged for baby-sitter — Kathy (15 and very reliable) next door, No. 47, daughter of Prof. Carson, Math, and very nice . . . feel free to call them if you need help of any kind. Extra blankets — top shelf bedroom closet . . . Bob attached side rail to Rachel's bed for Jonathan . . . No automatic switch for lights on Friday night. Bob and I are not that Orthodox. If you are, leave them on all night . . . Our good friend, Prof. Bill Richardson, Philosophy Department, was much taken with David's paper on Maimonides. He is holding open house in David's honor Saturday night. Did Bob mention it to David?''

Miriam poked her head in the living room and viewed her husband lying on the couch with affectionate annoyance. ''David!'' she called sharply. ''Sit up.''

"I took my shoes off," he protested.

"And how about your jacket? It will be all wrinkled for tonight."

"I'm wearing my black suit tonight. This will smooth out when I hang it up."

She sighed. "Did Bob say anything about a party Saturday night?"

"No, I don't think so."

"Well, there's going to be one in your honor. A Professor Richardson is having open house."

This time the rabbi swung his legs over and sat up. "I don't think I care for that. Besides, I was planning to drive back to Barnard's Crossing. I all but promised Mr. Wasserman."

"But it's for you, Nancy says. We'll have to go."

# 4

At the Malden bowling alley the manager reported a cracked plate-glass window. "It must have happened during the night, Mr. Paff. Everything was all right when I closed up. Then when I came to open this morning —"

"How come you opened this morning? Where's Hank?"

"Oh, yeah, I was going to tell you. Hank called me at the house and asked me to open for him. He wasn't feeling so good."

"Was he drunk?" Paff asked quickly.

"Gee, Mr. Paff, I wouldn't know about that. He just called and asked could I open and take the day shift. So I said all right. You know, he took my shift one night last week when I had that twenty-four-hour bug."

"All right. Get a wide piece of adhesive tape and tape that window up on both sides so there won't be any chance of it shattering. I'll notify the insurance company. Maybe they'll want to come out and take a look at it before I fix it."

"Sure, Mr. Paff. I'll do that right away," the manager assured him. "And can you get someone for the evening shift? I'll stay on if I have to, but it's a long day."

"Did you call the office?"

"I called, but there was no answer."

"Oh yeah, I forgot. I let the girl have the day off. All right, I'll swing by there and get the list and see what I can do."

At the Melrose alley Paff noticed that the gold leaf on the window sign was chipped and peeling near the corner. It made the golden bowling ball, which was the company's trademark, look like a reproving eye.

"When did that happen?" he asked the manager, pointing to the sign.

"What? The sign? It's always been like that, Mr. Paff."

35

"I never noticed."

"The pinsetting machines in the last two alleys got stuck again, Mr. Paff."

"Did you call the mechanic? You got the number."

"Yeah, I called him yesterday and again today. He says he'll be right over, but he said that yesterday."

"When did you call him today?" Paff asked.

"This morning, first thing when I came in."

"So call him again."

"Oh, I'll call him, but in the meantime we can't use the alleys."

"Those mechanics!" Paff shook his head. "Say, would you like to work an evening shift tonight — over in Malden?"

"Gee, Mr. Paff, I'd like to help you out, but the missus got something planned for tonight."

Business was off at the Medford alley. "It's this new billiard parlor that opened up in the shopping center," the manager explained. "Everybody's suddenly gone crazy over billiards. Even the dames. They come there and knit — can you imagine, knit? — waiting their turn to shoot."

Paff asked if he was free to work the evening shift over in Malden.

"You mean instead of working here? You planning to close this place down? Just because business is off for a couple of days?"

"No, I mean just for tonight, to sub."

"Oh, sure, anytime at all. Glad to help you out. Of course, Fridays I can't. I got this job Friday nights . . ."

He swung over to Chelsea, where his office was located, and only after he had finally found a place to park did he realize that he didn't have his office key.

The janitor was a new man and didn't know him.

"Look, here's my car license. See, I'm Meyer Paff. What more do you want?"

"Yeah, but you're asking me to open the office of the Golden Ball Enterprises. There's nothing on your license, mister, that shows you're connected with them."

Paff bit his lip in annoyance, although strict justice forced him to admit that the janitor was right. "I'm just going to make a couple of phone calls," he said. "You can stand right there while I do it."

"Sorry, mister, I got orders. The management is mighty strict about it. There's been a lot of breaks."

Paff tried to keep his voice calm. "Look, is Dr. Northcott still in his office, or has he gone to lunch? You know, the dentist on the third floor."

"I didn't see him go out."

"All right, take me up to him. He'll tell you who I am."

The dentist showed his annoyance at being called away from his patient, but he identified him.

It sure has been one of those days, Paff thought as he riffled through the card file. He dialed a number and sat with the instrument pressed to his ear as the phone rang and rang. Finally, he hung up and dialed another number. Again, the phone rang without eliciting a response. The third call, the phone was answered immediately. It was a woman. "No, Marty ain't home. Who shall I say called?" He didn't bother to explain.

With the next call, he was lucky. "I figured I'd be hearing from you, Mr. Paff. Hank called me on account I subbed for him a couple of weeks ago, and I said okay."

"Fine. Now look, there's a broken window, and I had Ted tape it with adhesive tape for the time being. I want you to check it before you close to make sure that tape is nice and secure. Okay?"

On his way out he stopped to thank the janitor and commend him for his caution. He pressed a couple of cigars on him.

"Thanks, Mr. — er —"

"Paff."

"Oh, yeah. Well thanks, Mr. Paff. I won't forget next time."

When he got back to his car, it was jammed in between two others. By the time he had extricated himself, he was bathed in perspiration. I'm getting too old for this, he thought. Then he remembered he hadn't had lunch. Glumly, he passed a nearby restaurant, noting the lot was full. He decided to eat on the road and stopped at a diner, where the only stool vacant was in front of the grill. Morosely watching the short order cook in a dirty apron, he managed to consume a dry hamburger and a cup of bad coffee.

# 5

In the Officers' Cafeteria of Hexatronics, Inc., on Route 128, there was a long middle table where the executives usually ate family-style, while on the sides there were a number of booths available for those who had guests and wished to talk in private. In a booth, Ted Brennerman studied the menu and said to his host, Ben Gorfinkle, "Hey, you guys do all right for yourselves." He gave his order, and as soon as the waitress left, he leaned across the table. "As I was saying, Ben, there's thirty-seven guys with nameplates on their seats in the sanctuary; there's another fifty or sixty get the same seats all the time — figure a hundred altogether. The rest of us — the peasants — sometimes we get a seat up front, and the next year we're way out in left field someplace. Last year I sat in the last row. So what difference did it make? With the public address system, I could hear just as good. But there are plenty others who don't feel like I do. They want to sit up front." He was a tall, good-looking young man, eager and with a ready, infectious smile.

"But they paid a special price for those seats. At least those with the nameplates did," Gorfinkle pointed out.

"Don't you believe it. I checked into it. I went back to the minutes of the general meeting of five years ago. What happened was they were putting on a drive for the Building Fund and getting all kinds of pledges. Then Becker, who was president that year, said that anyone who would donate a grand could have his seat reserved from year to year. Now, that wasn't anything the board had decided on and voted on. It was during the meeting and came out on the spur of the moment, if you see what I mean. Then" — he pressed Gorfinkle's arm for emphasis — "the board at their next meeting had to make some ruling to get Becker out of the jam he'd got himself into. So they said that those who had come forward with their thousand-buck donation would have their seats held until the last day of the ticket sale each year. But then the very next year they stopped selling seats anyway and made it part of the annual membership dues, so it seems to me that those guys don't have any kind of a claim on those cushy seats that they get year after year. And I'll tell you another thing: Not all of those guys who had nameplates put on their seats gave their thousand bucks."

Gorfinkle, a stocky, square-faced man in his mid-forties, said, "One of these days, we'll be putting in theater-type seats. Maybe we ought to wait till then."

"Nussbaum's project?" Brennerman laughed. "He came to see me right after I was elected president of the Brotherhood, I should have the Brotherhood start a drive for the additional money to put in new seats. And he spoke to me again only last week. He's bugged each of the Brotherhood presidents for the last four years, and the Sisterhood, too. I told him it wasn't anything I thought you could work up any enthusiasm for."

"I don't know, they're mighty uncomfortable. And we've got the money for about half the job."

"Yeah, it's a shame to think of that money lying there, and we can't touch it. Boy, if we could use that for the Social Action Fund! Say, maybe Mrs. Oppenheimer's will could be interpreted so at least we could use the money to buy upholstered pads for the present seats," Brennerman suggested.

Gorfinkle shook his head. "That wouldn't do any good. It would just make the seats higher, and they're too high as it is. It's not so much the seat part as the back. It's so straight or something. The only one who likes it is Doc Klein, the osteopath. He gets more leg cramp and sacroiliac business after Yom Kippur than he gets all year round."

Brennerman laughed. "Who picked that type seat in the first place?"

"Nobody picked it. They were so overwhelmed — most of them, those same people with the seat plates — by the reputation of that architect that they let

44

him do whatever he wanted. Those were copied from some Old English church, I understand. What did he care? He was just interested in how it looked; he wasn't going to have to sit in them. It's funny about this seat business. In the *shul* that my father used to go to, where you sat was a big deal. By tradition, the big shots, the guys with *yicchus,* status, always sat down front. The nearer you were to the ark, the more important you were. In that *shul* they even had a row of seats up against the wall where the ark was, facing the rest of the congregation. I remember the guys that sat there, most of them old guys with long beards, wearing these long woolen prayer shawls. My father called them *p'nai.* Gosh, I haven't thought of that word in years. It's a Hebrew word, and it means faces. My father used to explain to me that they were the faces of the congregation, the most pious and the most learned.''

"Well, I don't suppose we have any of those in our congregation unless maybe old man Goralsky and Wasserman.''

''I think maybe Meyer Paff

thinks he's one."

Both men chuckled.

"One thing bothers me, though," Gorfinkle went on. "I still think that this kind of thing — announcing a whole new social action program for the temple — ought to be presented at the general meeting of the congregation. When you come right down to it, we haven't even formally presented it to the board."

"Hell, we campaigned on it, Ben. So it's no secret. And since we've a majority, we've got a right to run things our way."

"Still —"

"And don't you see," said the other eagerly, "presenting it at the Brotherhood service — that's the beauty of it. For one thing, we'll have more people there than we ever get at a general meeting. The last meeting we only got a little over a hundred. We get close to three times that at the Brotherhood service. And with the rabbi away, we won't have to worry about anything he might say afterward."

Gorfinkle chuckled. "And he doesn't know it yet, but he won't be there for the meeting Sunday either."

"No? How come?"

"Well, he expected to drive home right after the evening service Saturday, but they're having a kind of party for him Saturday night at the college, according to Stu. He won't be able to leave until Sunday morning. After all, they've got the kid with them."

"Good thinking."

"But it's not the rabbi I'm worried about; it's Paff."

The younger man grinned. "Well, don't worry about Paff. I've got an idea how to take care of him."

# 6

There were no customers present, and Meyer Paff looked around uncertainly for a moment and then made his way to the rear of the store, where Mr. Begg sat glowering at him.

"I'm Meyer Paff," he said. "Mr. Morehead said you had the key to the Hillson place, that you were like a caretaker —"

"I live in the carriage house. I keep an eye on the place," said Begg evenly.

Meyer Paff was a big, slow-moving man. Everything about him was big: his large round head surmounted by a tuft of blondish-gray hair, his fleshy nose, the square, chalky teeth, the big red hands with sausagelike fingers, the feet encased in badly turned shoes, as though the leather was not strong enough to contain them. When he spoke, it was in a deep bass burble, with the large red lips scarcely moving, so that the sound seemed to come not so much from the mouth as from the belly. Nevertheless, he felt ill at ease before the stare of the other man.

"Morehead said he called you —"

"I spoke to him on the phone this morning."

"So if I can have the key —"

Begg did not answer but leaned forward and from somewhere under the kneehole of the desk brought out a cardboard on which was a crayoned message: BACK IN ONE HOUR.

"Oh, there's no need for you to leave your store. If you just give me —"

"The house is furnished, and I don't give the key out to strangers," he said flatly. When he saw Paff redden, he added, "No business this time of day, anyway. You got a car? Then you follow me."

Hillson House and the carriage house nearby were built on the promontory known as Tarlow's Point and were set back about forty feet from the street line, the only two houses on the street for some distance. A high, thick hedge all but concealed the front lawn and then continued along the side of the lot to merge with a stand of straggly pines leading to the beach and the water.

Paff pointed beyond the hedge to a narrow path leading down to the water. "Is that part of the estate?" he asked.

"Well, it is and it isn't. It's part of the lot, but it's a public right-of-way. The Hillsons have been fighting with the town about it off and on for a number of years."

"Then it's not a private beach?"

"Well, the Hillsons claim it is. The town says that this vacant lot across the street" — he motioned with his chin — "has access rights to the beach. But then the Hillsons went and bought that lot some years ago, so it would seem that the whole of Tarlow's Point is theirs. But the town council says no, because they could sell that lot separately and the new owner would have access rights."

"I see."

Begg led the way to the front door.

"They selling the whole business?" he asked.

"That's what I understand."

The door opened into a short vestibule, beyond which was a large living room. There were three windows, two facing the front lawn and the third on the side facing the carriage house, all hung with lace curtains and heavy, old-fashioned red velvet drapes with valances at the top and drawn back halfway down by a loop of the same material. The furniture was covered with large sheets of heavy plastic, but from what could be seen through them, it seemed of a piece with the velvet drapes — heavy, overstuffed sofas, chairs upholstered in damask, and heavy, clumsy mahogany tables.

"This was used as a summer home? The furniture isn't what you'd expect —"

"I guess they had it originally in their house in Cambridge. Folks didn't throw out good furniture in those days."

Begg led Paff down a hall that ran toward the back of the house, opening doors on either side on the way. The first door revealed a small study with a couch, shelves of books, a couple of chairs, and a flat-topped desk. Like the furniture in the living room, the couch and desk were covered with plastic throws. The other rooms were bedrooms, and in each case the bed at least was covered with a plastic sheet. Paff rapped on the wall. "Is this a supporting wall?" he asked.

"I don't think so."

There was a large inkblot on one of the walls of the far bedroom. Paff pointed at it. "One of the Hillsons have a bad temper?"

"Vandals," replied Begg shortly. "A couple of years back the high school kids took to breaking into some of these summer homes, pinching things, raising hell generally. That's how I happened to get this job. You want to see the upstairs?"

"I don't think so."

They were in the kitchen now, and from the windows through the stand of pines they could see the ocean. "The tide is out now," Begg said, "but when it's in, the water comes right up to the sea wall and cuts the Point off from the rest of the beach."

"Comes up pretty high, does it?"

"Oh, at least a couple or three feet."

From the front of the house the ground sloped away to the beach so that there was a flight of a dozen or more steps leading down from the back door. "Can we look at the place from in back?"

"Look, mister, I got a business back in town."

"Oh, sure," said Paff. "Well, you can just go on ahead. I'll look around by myself."

"Suit yourself." He opened the door, and Paff started down the stairs. Begg locked the door behind him and went out the front to his car.

Paff got as far as the trees and then turned around to face the house. I'll have to come back with a tape and take some measurements, he thought. Maybe bring an architect along. Take out those inside walls. Might have to put beams up, though. I could have a kitchen to one side or upstairs and use a dumbwaiter, and the rest of the place could be tables and booths. I could put up a Quonset hut against the rear for the alleys. It would mean going down a flight of stairs to the alleys, but it would make it quieter in the dining area. With windows all around, you could see the ocean, and it would be nice and cool all through the summer. I could blacktop the lot across the street . . .

He returned to his car and debated whether to go to Lynn or Gloucester. Lynn was nearer, but Gloucester involved a long, pleasant drive along the shore road, and he felt he could use the relaxation. The manager of the Gloucester alley had nothing unusual to report; everything was going along smoothly.

"You sure nothing's wrong?"

"What's the matter, Mr. Paff? Don't you think I can run the place? Let me tell you —"

"No, that's all right, Jim. It's just that I've had one of those days when everyplace I went — Know what I mean?"

"Oh, sure. You through now?"

"Just Lynn, and then I'll go on home. I covered some of the places yesterday."

"Well, have a nice weekend, Mr. Paff.

And don't worry."

The Lynn alley was empty when he arrived, save for the manager, who was leaning on the counter, puffing on a cigar.

"Slow day, Henry?"

"This time just before supper is always slow, Mr. Paff. You usually get here earlier."

"I did Gloucester first. Everything all right? Those ashtrays look pretty full —"

"I'm just taking a breather for five or ten minutes. We'll get a rush in about half an hour."

"You go off in an hour."

"Yeah, if Moose gets here on time. So far, he's been late every night this week."

He stiffened as a car drove up and a couple of men got out and headed for the door. "Fuzz," he whispered.

"Here? What do they want? What's the matter?"

"H'lo boys," Henry greeted the plainclothesmen. "You want to bowl a couple of strings?"

"Not today, Henry. We just want to look over the joint." One strode purposefully toward the little ell where the toilets were situated. Henry came from behind the counter to watch him. He stopped in front of the door marked LADIES.

"Anybody in here?" he asked.

"No, but you can't go in there," said Henry indignantly.

"Why not?"

"Can't you read? That's the ladies' john."

"So I'm feeling girlish." He opened the door and went inside.

The other man had dumped one of the ashtrays onto the floor and squatted down to inspect the contents. Paff came over. "Look here," he said. "What's all this about?"

"Who're you, mister?"

"I'm Meyer Paff. I own the place."

"Do you mind standing back; you're in my light." He straightened up and went to the next lane to inspect the ashtrays there. "Police business," he said. "We got a tip, so we're checking it. You around here much?"

"Well, I — I come in a couple of times a week maybe. Sometimes only once."

56

"You don't mind how you mess up a place," said Henry. "You going to leave that stuff there?"

"Sure, we'll leave it for the sweeper."

"You guys got a search warrant?" demanded Henry.

"No, no," said Paff. "Never mind, Henry —"

The policeman looked at the manager in surprise. "What do we need a search warrant for? It's a public place, and my partner had to go to the john."

"Not to the ladies' john."

"Please, Henry." Paff turned to the policeman. "Look, do you mind telling me what you're looking for?"

"We're looking for pot, mister."

"But why here?"

The other policeman joined them, shaking his head in response to his partner's look of inquiry.

"Well, we got a tip, so we checked it through. You ever see any kids acting high?" he demanded of Henry.

"The little bastards all act high," said Henry indignantly. "That still don't give you no call to come down here —"

"Without a search warrant? Look, Buster, we come down here *with* a warrant, we take the place apart."

"No need to get excited, Officer," said Paff. "We're always happy to cooperate with the police."

"Yeah? Well, tell your man."

When he got home, Mrs. Paff greeted him at the door with, "Where were you? It's so late I was beginning to worry. Hurry and wash up. Dinner has been ready for half an hour."

"I don't feel like eating now, Laura. I'm tired. I'll eat later."

"But we've got to go to the temple, Meyer. It's Friday night."

"I think I'll pass it up tonight. I'm tired."

"Come on, Meyer, sit down and eat something, and you'll feel better. And then we'll go to the temple, and you can relax. It's the Brotherhood service. You always enjoy that."

# 7

As Ted Brennerman strode to the pulpit the congregation settled back expectantly. He had a reputation as a "hot-shot" and a "character." ("That Brennerman, he doesn't care what he says; he gets away with murder.") Leaning against the lectern in a manner obviously reminiscent of Rabbi Small, he announced, "Good evening, this is your friendly Rabbi Brennerman." There was a titter of appreciation, and he went on, "Seriously, folks, I've done a lot of public talking in my time, but this is the first time I've had to give a sermon. Let me tell you, it sobers a fellow up." There was another appreciative chuckle, for among the Brotherhood members Brennerman was reputed to know what to do with a bottle.

"So when I found that the program

called for me to give the sermon, I asked our rabbi if I could borrow his sermon book. (Laughter.) Well, he claimed he didn't have one, that he made them up himself. So I thought to myself, I know what to get *you* for your birthday. (Laughter.) Actually, no one here has a greater appreciation of our rabbi than I have. I consider him one of the wisest and most intelligent men I've met. And I guess he proved it when he arranged to play hookey tonight. (Laughter.)

"So since I didn't get any help from our rabbi, I went over his head and consulted his boss, Moses himself. Always deal with the top man is my motto. I took down the family Bible and began to read in Exodus. I read it in English, because I didn't happen to have my Hebrew glasses around. (Laughter.) Well, it was a revelation. And there's no pun intended. We all know the story of the exodus from Egypt, the ten plagues, and all the rest of it from way back in Sunday school. But when you read it in the Bible, you really get an idea of what clowns Pharaoh and the Egyptians were. And I guess recent events in the Middle East tend to prove that they haven't wised up very much in three thousand years. (Appreciative laughter.) Except that *then* they wanted us to stay, and *now* they want us to get out. Can't they make up their minds what they want? (Laughter.)

"But then as I continued reading I discovered that our own folks weren't an awful lot brighter. Get the picture: They had just been treated to as classy a demonstration of God's power as had ever been displayed to mankind. Again and again, God had demonstrated that He regarded the children of Israel with special favor. He had plagued the land with flies and with locusts, with darkness and with death, and in each case the Israelites got off scot-free. Did they need any more proof positive? He gave it to them: He parted the waters of the Red Sea to let them pass. How did the Israelites react? You'd think that after all that they'd be four-square behind Moses. But no, as soon as they realized the Egyptians were after them, some of them — I'm sure it wasn't all of them — began to crack wise at his expense. 'Did you take us out here to die in the wilderness because they didn't have any graves in Egypt?' And to the other Israelites they said, 'Don't you remember? I told you we ought to stay in Egypt and serve the Egyptians. It's better than dying in the wilderness.' Now you all know God's answer to that. When the Egyptians came along, He rolled the waters of the sea back again and drowned the lot of them.

"Did that end the griping? Did that end the doubt? Not by a long shot. It happened again and again. Anytime the situation wasn't a hundred percent kosher, this bunch — and I'm sure it was the same bunch all the time — would begin acting up. It happened when they got to Marah and the available water was bitter. And again later on when rations were low and they yearned for the fleshpots of Egypt. That was when God sent down manna from the heavens. And later on when they ran out of water and they thought God was going to let them die of thirst. That was the time that Moses struck the rock with his rod and produced water. And then it happened again when Moses went up on the mount to receive the tables of the Law. When he didn't come down right away, they were sure they had been abandoned, and they forced Aaron to make them an image of a golden calf so they could worship it."

Brennerman's tone had changed, and the congregation was giving him its full attention. "Now Moses had given them a set of laws. These weren't laws of ritual and prayer; they were laws to live by, the laws necessary to maintain a workable society. It was a primitive society they had in those days, and they needed some pretty elementary ethical rules to make it work, laws like 'Thou shalt not kill' and 'Thou shalt not steal' and 'Thou shalt not bear false witness.' We all know that you can't have a society where murder and stealing and bearing false witness are permitted or condoned. It would disintegrate overnight. Those laws were necessary for the society of that time to maintain itself and to grow and prosper. And isn't that what our religion is essentially — a set of rules that men can live by?

"But now we live in a more complex society, and that calls for different rules, or perhaps for a new interpretation of the old rules. We know now that when large segments of our population have inadequate food and clothing and shelter — that is a form of murder. When we prevent the Negro from stating his case and protesting his true predicament, that is a form of bearing false witness. That when our young men are not permitted to listen to the voices of their own conscience and we force them to do the will of the majority, then you are setting up another god, the god of the Establishment. What I'm saying is that the true function of a temple — or a church, for that matter — is to see that the society of its time is workable, and in these days that means taking the lead in matters like civil rights and social justice and international peace."

Brennerman adjusted his yarmulke on his head. "I would like to see our temple take a positive stand on all these matters and make our voice heard. I would like to see our temple pass resolutions on these matters and then notify the daily press of our stand and send copies to the state legislature and to our representatives in Congress.

"And I would have us do more. When our Negro brothers picket for social justice, I would like to see a team from this temple right there with them. And when there are hearings held on various social matters, I would like to see a group from this temple down at the hearing room making it plain that we regard these as religious matters.

"What's more, I would like us to appropriate monies to be set aside in a special Social Action Fund so that we could make contributions — as a temple — to various worthy causes, like the Poverty March on Washington, legal aid for political prisoners in the South, and yes, even on occasion to support candidates for public office who represent our views and who are running against opponents who are known reactionaries and bigots.

"My attitude on this is no secret and

comes as no surprise to you, because it is the platform on which I campaigned for the presidency of the Brotherhood, and it is the platform on which the present administration of the temple campaigned. And the fact of our election indicates that the majority of the congregation agrees with us and has given us a mandate to go ahead. And our platform can be stated in a few words: The job of the temple is to help make democracy work.

"As I said, none of this is a surprise to you, because we have been urging it all along. But it is one thing to urge and another to implement. So tonight I would like to announce the first step in our new temple program. We feel that democracy should start at home. So instead of the old system of reserved seats where the best ones always went to the same few individuals, we are going to institute a system of no reservations in the sanctuary, with seating on a first-come, first-served basis. Our president, Ben Gorfinkle, felt it only fitting that I should make the announcement, since the Brotherhood furnishes the ushers for the High Holidays.''

There was an excited buzzing in the congregation. But Brennerman went on. ''Now, I know that not every member of the congregation or of the Brotherhood, for that matter, agrees with us on our idea of the function of a temple. I know that there are those who feel that a temple should be just a place where you go to recite prayers and go through ritual motions. I think they are the same kind of people who were worried when Moses went up on the mountain and insisted that Aaron make the golden calf. They are the people who are not interested in a real commitment, who are afraid of getting involved in controversy. What they want is a religion where you go through a bunch of religious motions. I consider that akin to the worship of the golden Paff — I mean calf. (Loud sniggers.) And I consider that golden'' — he paused, as if to make sure that this time he got it right —''calf religion.'' He went on for some minutes longer, comparing what he called real religion and calf religion. And each time he was exaggeratedly careful of his pronunciation. He ended up with a call for unity "so we can make this the best religious organization on the North Shore."

He returned to his seat beside Gorfinkle, who rose and gravely offered him the customary congratulatory handshake. But after they were seated again, behind the concealment of his prayer book, Gorfinkle touched the tip of his forefinger to his thumb to form an *O* to indicate his unqualified approval.

# 8

"Hello there, Hughie m'boy. 'Tis your old friend Kevin O'Connor."

"Uh-huh." Hugh Lanigan, chief of the Barnard's Crossing police force, did not like to be called Hughie, and he did not particularly like Kevin O'Connor, chief of the neighboring Lynn force. He regarded him as a professional Irishman, even a stage Irishman, since he was American-born and the brogue obviously was put on. The most he would allow was that it might have political advantages in Lynn.

"You'll be going to the Police Chiefs' spring dance, won't you, Hughie?"

"Haven't made up my mind yet."

"Well, I wish you'd let me put your name down now. I'm on the committee, and I'd like to make a good showing."

"I'll let you know, Kevin."

"You don't have to send in the form." Lanigan was amused to note all traces of brogue had vanished. "Just give me a call, and I'll be happy to put your name down, and you can send me the money anytime you think of it."

"Okay, Kevin."

But the other was not yet finished. "Oh, and by the by, would you happen to be knowing an individual name of Paff, a resident of your lovely town, a kind of a Jew type?"

"Meyer Paff?"

"That's the one."

"Yes, I know him," said Lanigan cautiously. "What do you want to know about him?"

"Oh, just the usual. Is he a respectable citizen? Have you ever had any dealings with him — in the way of business, you might say."

"He's well thought of here in town. No police record of any kind, if that's what you mean. What's he done?" But already Lanigan had scribbled the name on a memorandum pad.

"Well now, I don't know that he's done

anything. But he owns a bowling alley here."

"He owns half a dozen in cities and towns along the North Shore," said Lanigan.

"I know, but none in Barnard's Crossing." It sounded like an accusation.

"We don't have one here, but the one in Salem is near enough. What's wrong with the bowling alley in Lynn?"

"Well," said O'Connor, "some of the kids who have been smoking pot and have given us a little trouble, that's one of their regular hangouts."

"And you think he might be pushing the stuff?" Lanigan scratched out the name on the pad. "I can't picture him in the part. He's one of the big shots in the local temple, for one thing."

"Well now, Hughie, did you ever think that might be a kind of cover-up?"

"No, I haven't, but I'll think about it — when I've nothing better to do."

"You'll have your little joke, won't you. And down there, aren't you troubled with it?"

"With pot? We've had some," said

Lanigan cautiously. "As near as we can make out, it seems to be coming in from Boston."

"Well, if anything comes to you, any bit of gossip about this Paff, I'd appreciate your letting me know."

"Ye can bank on it, Kevin m'boy." Lanigan banged the receiver down and glared at the instrument for a moment. Then he chuckled.

# 9

"Nice sermon, Ted," said Meyer Paff. Most of the congregation had already filed out of the sanctuary to go down to the vestry, where a collation had been prepared. Paff, standing athwart the middle aisle, had waited for Brennerman and Gorfinkle, who were making their way from the pulpit.

"Did you really like it?" asked Brennerman eagerly, too eagerly.

"Sure, I liked it fine," Paff said in his deep rumble. "All through it I was thinking — here we're paying the rabbi a big salary. For what? To give sermons mostly. The rest of his job — making little speeches to the Bar Mitzvahs, marrying people, visiting the sick — we could have the cantor do it or the president. The one thing was the sermons. And now you prove that any fresh young punk can do just as well."

"Now look here —"

"This is no place to pick a fight, Meyer," said Gorfinkle quietly.

"Who's fighting?" Several tailenders of the congregation filing out stopped to listen. "Would I fight in the sanctuary? Believe me, I wasn't brought up that way. I'd as soon get up in the pulpit and insult one of the members."

"Insult? Who was insulted?" asked Gorfinkle.

"I don't know. Maybe Doc Edelstein. He doesn't favor the temple getting into politics. I doubt he cared much for being called an idol worshiper. Or maybe he doesn't know any better. He always thought he was a good Jew. He helped start this place and gave a lot of money to get it going. My friend Irving Kallen, he wasn't here tonight, but he gave a lot of money, too, for this temple. And maybe you don't know it but the Kallen Family Fund has made a contribution to the NAACP for years. But Irv Kallen never suggested that because he wanted to, I had to.

"You were talking about some of the seats that have little nameplates on them. I don't suppose you happened to notice, but on that stand you were talking from and on the reader's desk behind you and on the very chair you were sitting on, there was a little brass plate telling that it was contributed by the Kallen Family Fund, all the pulpit furniture, including the ark and the public address system you were talking through. Maybe he wouldn't have been in such a hurry to give it if he had known some young wise guy was going to use it to call him a worshiper of the golden calf."

"Money isn't everything," said Gorfinkle, "and it doesn't give you the right —"

"Sure, I know money isn't everything. Some people can talk and make speeches instead. I didn't go to college like you boys. I grew up in the streets, but I learned a couple of things there. One was talk is cheap. And when some wise guy would sound off about something he claimed to know for sure, we would say,

75

'Put your money where your mouth is.' "

"Well, let me tell you —"

"I just want to ask you one question, Ted. It's about your sermon. I'm not going to ask you what the purpose of it was. That was pretty clear: The temple is growing; it's getting too big for the both of us. Maybe you think it would be better for all concerned if you cut it down some in size."

"I didn't —"

"No, what I want to ask you is, in your sermon, in laying down the law the way you did, did you think of yourself as Moses? Or God?"

# 10

There were less than twenty-five present Friday evening in the tiny Hillel House chapel, and Rabbi Small suspected that some of them were Gentiles. One who sat well in back certainly was not Jewish, since he was dressed in black and wore a Roman collar. The rabbi assumed he was the director of the Newman Club at the college, and so it turned out when he approached him at the end of the service and introduced himself. Father Bennett was a youngish-looking man of thirty, slim and boyish, and he laughed easily.

"Scouting the opposition, Father?" the rabbi teased.

The priest laughed. "For a while, I thought you might need me to round out your minyan. Is that the word?"

"That's the word. The attendance was

rather disappointing.''

''Actually, I'm surprised you got as many as you did. The great majority of students left this afternoon or earlier — right after their last class. Not that Rabbi Dorfman draws crowds, you understand. For that matter, I figure I am getting only about a quarter of the students I should,'' he added hastily, as if to avoid any disparagement of Rabbi Dorfman. ''In our case, it's understandable: The church is in a state of flux; we're trying to modernize. But so many of our young people are holding back, as though waiting to see which road the church will take. They don't accept blindly; they question and discuss and argue.''

''And you find this disturbing?''

''Not at all,'' said the priest quickly. ''But much that they question we are not in a position to answer. Take the matter of birth control. So many of our Catholic students come from large families. In most cases, they are the first of their families to go to college. Well, you know from hearing them talk that they aren't planning to have six or seven children; two or three at the most, and that means birth control.''

''Well?''

''Of course, upper-income Catholics have been doing it for years. In the higher social levels the large family is the exception, rather than the rule. But these young people are frightfully sincere. If the church establishes a regulation that runs counter to their common sense, they won't just disregard it, as other generations have done. They're more apt to disassociate themselves from the church completely.''

''Young people grow wiser or at least more tolerant as they grow older,'' said the rabbi.

''Perhaps,'' said Father Bennett, ''although frankly, I'm hoping the church will grow more tolerant, too. On this matter of birth control, for instance, the committee the Pope set up to study the question, opinion was overwhelmingly in favor of permitting the use of the pill.''

''But the Pope has come out against the pill.''

''For the present, yes. But there's a good chance one of these days he may change the doctrine.''

The rabbi shook his head. "He can't. He really can't.''

The priest smiled. "It's not a dogma, you know, and the church is a very human institution.''

"It's also a very logical institution, and the question of birth control impinges on the sanctity of marriage, which *is* a dogma.''

"And what is your position?''

"Well, we regard monogamous marriage as a highly artificial institution which is nevertheless the best system we have for organizing society. It is like a legal contract, which can be broken by divorce in the event that it becomes impossible for the two principals to continue. But with you, marriage is a sacrament and marriages are made in heaven. You can't permit divorce, because that would suggest that heaven had erred, and that is unthinkable. The best you can afford is annulment — a kind of legal fiction that it never happened.''

They had left Hillel House and were strolling along the neat campus walk. Now they had arrived in front of the Dorfman home. "And how do you see birth control affecting our teaching on marriage?" asked Father Bennett.

"It becomes a question of what the function of marriage is," said the rabbi. "If it is procreation, then I suppose it makes sense to consider it the business of heaven. But it is hard to imagine heaven being greatly concerned with an institution that is largely intended for recreation. And that would be the effect if the use of the pill were condoned."

When Father Bennett had left them and the baby-sitter had departed and they were alone together, Miriam asked, "What got into you tonight, David? Were you deliberately baiting that nice Father Bennett?"

He looked at her in surprise and then grinned. "I suppose it's hardly the sort of discussion I would be likely to hold with Father Burke in Barnard's Crossing. Somehow I feel freer here. Perhaps it's the academic atmosphere. Do you think he was annoyed?"

"I don't know," she answered. "If he

was, he took it well."

Professor Richardson lived in an old Victorian house. A large, square vestibule was separated by sliding doors from the living room, at the other end of which was another pair of sliding doors, which led to the dining room. Both pairs of doors had been pushed back to form one huge L-shaped room. By nine Saturday night the party was in full swing. People were standing around in small groups sipping their drinks. At one end of the room several chairs were clustered around a small table where the rabbi and Mrs. Small were sitting with their host, Professor Richardson, a youngish-looking, athletic man who kept interrupting his conversation with the rabbi to jump up to greet some new arrival, whom he would bring over to present. Mrs. Richardson circulated among her guests with occasional hasty forays into the kitchen to replenish the supply of food and drinks.

Invariably there were questions: "Why do you people wear that shawl thing with the fringed edges at your services?" "Do you have to have ten men in order to pray?" "Those dietary laws you people have — they were a health measure, weren't they? Why do you need them now that we have modern methods of refrigeration?" "What's being done to bring the synagogue up to date?"

Most of the older people, faculty members, made a point of coming over; and they, too, asked questions, meaningless, polite questions, intended only to make conversation: "You from around here, Rabbi?" "How do you like our school?" "You taking Bob Dorfman's place?"

On the other hand, the majority of the young people, he soon saw, had come not to meet him, but one another. They stood around in small groups; in one corner six or eight were sitting on the floor, one of them lying on his belly, his feet in worn moccasins waving in the air. From their intent expressions punctuated by explosive laughter, he gathered they were telling jokes, off-color jokes probably. Some of those who did approach him apologized for having missed the service the night before. When the student president of Hillel slid into the chair beside him, the rabbi remarked on it. The youth nodded. "You know how it is, Rabbi. No matter how you dress it up in your publicity, it's still a religious service. But an open house like this is a party. You can take a girl to something like this, and it constitutes a date. Understand?"

A tall, ungainly student with blondish hair approached. "H'lo, Rabbi, Mrs. Small." It was Stuart Gorfinkle.

"Oh, Stu, we've been trying to get you," said the rabbi.

"Yes, we phoned a couple of times," said Miriam, "and left a message."

"Yeah, I got it. Sorry I couldn't make it to the Hillel service last night. I had a date."

"That's all right," said the rabbi. "Are you driving home with us? We plan to leave about nine tomorrow morning."

"Well, it's like this, Rabbi. A couple of guys who live in Gloucester are leaving tonight, and they offered me a lift —"

He seemed embarrassed, so the rabbi said quickly, "Of course, Stuart."

"Well — say, I thought I'd drop in to see you some time tomorrow afternoon if you're going to be home." The young man sat down.

"By all means. We're expecting the students who are back from school."

Father Bennett came up and took a vacant chair beside the rabbi. He glanced at Stuart and half nodded, as though not sure whether he knew him or not. He smiled at Miriam.

"Do I have to apologize to you, Father?" asked the rabbi. "My wife thought I was baiting you last night."

"Oh, really?" He laughed. "Of course, you realize, Mrs. Small, that your husband is a Jesuit. Myself, I'm not very strong in the hairsplittings of theological argument. You have a name for that sort of reasoning, don't you, Rabbi?"

"Pilpul," said the rabbi, "although I think you will find it somewhat different from Jesuitical disciplines."

"Perhaps not," said Father Bennett. "But, as my young people say, each person must do his thing, and mine is essentially counseling. I try to instill in my people a simple faith, and I leave all the subtleties to the big guns of the church. My feeling is that once a person has faith, then everything else falls into line. Since we're all pretty much in agreement on that, I consider it my contribution to the ecumenical spirit."

The rabbi coughed apologetically. "Well, not quite. There's a difference in orientation. You Catholics are heaven-oriented, while we Jews are content with this world. There was a saint in the Middle Ages who never laughed —"

The priest nodded. " 'My Savior is crucified, and shall I laugh?' "

"That's the one. And it's actually a logical attitude in the light of your theology. You aspire to sainthood. We are content with the human level. Of course," he added, "is isn't because we lack fervor or aspiration. Rather, we believe that if you aspire to something above the human level, there is grave danger of falling below it."

"But faith, Rabbi. If you have faith in the majesty and glory of God —"

"Ah, but we don't —"

"No faith?" The priest was shocked.

"None that is enjoined upon us. It is not a requirement of our religion, as it is of yours. I suspect it's a kind of special talent that some have to a greater degree than others. Basically, our thinking is in line with the passage from Micah: 'What doth the Lord require of thee but to walk in His way?' "

"Isn't that the same thing?"

"Not really. You can walk in His way and still have doubts of His existence. After all, you can't always control your thoughts. When you affirm your belief, doesn't that imply that just prior to your affirmation you doubted? Our doubts are not accompanied by feelings of guilt and terror that afflict your people. Psychologically, I suppose, it's healthier."

"And you, Rabbi, do you believe?"

The rabbi smiled. "I suspect that like you or anyone else for that matter, sometimes I do and sometimes I don't."

Stuart rose. "I got to split now, Rabbi. We'll be starting out pretty soon. See you tomorrow maybe?" He nodded uncertainly at the priest.

"Sure, Stuart."

"Drive carefully," said Miriam.

The rabbi looked around him and remarked that almost all the young people had gone. He turned to Miriam and then said to Father Bennett, "I think maybe —"

Just then Professor Richardson came over. "Oh, you can't go now, Rabbi. We're expecting Lucius Rathbone — oh, there he is now." He hurried off to greet the newcomer.

"Lucius Rathbone?"

"The poet," Father Bennett explained. *"Songs of the Ghetto. Blue Notes.* He's our poet in residence. Bill Richardson said he might be coming over."

The rabbi looked curiously toward the door and saw a tall, light-skinned Negro of forty, resplendent in a white turtleneck jersey and a black silk Nehru jacket. From his neck hung a silver chain and medallion, which he fingered. Beneath his pencil-line moustache, and above his little goatee he flashed strong white teeth in momentary smiles of greeting as Richardson, with one hand on his elbow, steered him across the room. His head held back, he looked down his aquiline nose from under lidded eyes as Richardson talked.

They came over. "Rabbi Small filled in for Bob Dorfman this week, Lucius. Mrs. Small, Rabbi, Lucius Rathbone."

The poet extended a hand and permitted the rabbi to press it. Still clutching the Negro, Richardson put an arm around the rabbi's shoulder. "Now that the youngsters are gone, Rabbi, we can all have a quiet cup of coffee around the table."

"We really ought to go, professor. We have a baby-sitter —"

"Surely you've got time for a cup of coffee."

The rabbi allowed himself to be persuaded. There were around a dozen seated at the table, and the talk was addressed largely to the poet.

"You working on something special right now, Lucius?"

"What about Prex's statement on the Student Afro-American League?"

"You hear anything about a new

department of urban sociology, Lucius?"

It was obvious to the rabbi that they had come not to greet him, but in the hope and expectation of meeting the poet. And it was just as obvious that he enjoyed their attention. He fielded their questions sometimes sarcastically, sometimes even caustically, but always with peremptory authority. And when on occasion his answer embarrassed the questioner, he tossed his head back and laughed hugely, as if to make it clear that no real animus was intended. It was a kind of game he was playing with them. When he noticed the rabbi glancing at his watch, he called across the table, "You're not planning on leaving now, are you, Rabbi?" as though resenting the idea.

"I'm afraid we have to —"

The poet's face took on a cunning look. "You know, my uncle was a rabbi."

"Is that so?" said the rabbi, although he knew he was being drawn.

Rathbone's voice shifted suddenly to a higher pitch, almost a falsetto, and he spoke in the street dialect of the Negro ghetto. "Leastways, that's what we called him. He was a preacher and had a storefront church he called Temple of Zion. Reverend Lucius Harper. I was named after him. We always called him Rabbi Harper. My old daddy said it was a religion he made up so's he could grease up to the Jew landlord who owned the building and maybe get free rent. But Rabbi Harper claimed as how he did it under conviction and that us poor colored folk would be better off if we stuck with the Old Testament. What do you think of that?"

"Naturally, I think you would," said the rabbi.

"Yeah? Then how come all the stores down in our neighborhood that were profiteering on us were owned by Jews?"

"Now, Lucius —" Professor Richardson was distressed.

A spot of color appeared in the rabbi's normally pale cheek. He said quietly, "I know only one Jewish merchant who had a store in the Negro area in the town where I grew up. His father had started it long before your people moved to the neighborhood. He was certainly not a rich man. He couldn't sell the store, and he never had the money to close up and start another in a different location. Finally the decision was made for him when there was a riot in the area. They broke his windows and cleaned out his shelves for him."

The Negro was not abashed; on the contrary, he glared at the rabbi, and when he spoke, it was once again in his normal cultured baritone, and his tone was accusing. "And am I supposed to feel shocked because my people finally kicked over the traces and got a little of their own back? For four hundred years you have oppressed us and brutalized us and enslaved us, robbed us of our heritage and our manhood —"

The rabbi rose, and Miriam, too, got up. "We really have to go, Mrs. Richardson." He turned to the Negro poet. "Those four hundred years you speak of, Mr. Rathbone, my people lived in the ghettos of Europe — Poland, Russia, Germany — and there were no Negroes there. My grandfather, who came to this country from a small town in Russia at the turn of the century, like the rest of my ancestors, had never even seen a Negro, much less enslaved and brutalized and robbed him of his manhood.'' Miriam had come over to stand beside her husband, and he took her arm. Now he stared directly into the angry eyes of the handsome, light-skinned Negro. "Can you say the same of your ancestors, Mr. Rathbone?"

# 11

"You whipsawed me," said Irving Kallen ruefully. "You and the Doc between you."

Meyer Paff grinned. "Nothing to it, Irving," he said. "It was the last hand, so we were just trying to make a pot."

"Don't you believe him, Irving," said Dr. Edelstein. He was a round man with a perpetual smile ("A natural bedside manner," his patients would say). "Normal tactics — drive out the buttonhole makers."

"You ended up ahead, didn't you?" demanded Paff.

Kallen evened off the little columns of chips in front of him. "Nope. Let's see, I'm down thirty-two, no, thirty-seven cents. You're the big winner tonight — as usual."

Paff gathered in the chips to put away in the box.

"Luck," said Kallen.

"Don't you believe it, Irv. You've got to know how to play," said Paff.

"Maybe you're right, Meyer. My game is bridge."

"If you got card sense," Kermit Arons offered, "you can play any card game."

"Well, last night, I was playing bridge over at Nelson Shaffer's house —"

"That explains it," said Paff with finality. "You go playing cards on the Sabbath instead of going to the temple, and the next time you play, you're going to lose."

"Well, for thirty-two, no thirty-seven cents, I figure I wasn't punished too bad. Taking the two nights together, I'm still wa-ay ahead of the game. And from what I heard," he added maliciously, "I'll bet you wish you hadn't gone last night."

Paff shrugged his shoulders.

"What Brennerman pulled on Meyer was pretty raw," said Arons, "but actually it was directed against all of us here."

"You mean the business of the seating?" asked Dr. Edelstein. "As far as I'm concerned, I'd just as soon sit in the back row. With the public address system, you can hear just as good, and to tell the truth I kind of like the idea of being near the door so I can go out for a breather every now and then without everybody noticing."

"How about if you find yourself downstairs in the vestry?"

"What do you mean?"

"Last year we had to have two services, one in the vestry. Right?"

"Yes, but the new members were assigned seats downstairs; the old members —"

"Sure, but the whole idea now is to make the seating democratic. If there are no reserved seats, it means that if you come in a little late, you go down to the vestry because all the seats in the sanctuary are full."

"I don't think I'd care for that."

"Well," said Kallen, "I don't like to sit in the back. What's more, my old man considers our seats in the first row a kind of honor."

"And how about the money we paid for those seats?" demanded Arons. "I plunked down a thousand bucks to the Building Fund — not a pledge, but hard cash — back when Becker was president. And it was supposed to reserve my seat for me each year, the same seat, mind you, until the last day of the ticket selling. Well now, I regard that as a contract that I entered into with the temple, and if anybody should live up to their contract, it seems to me it should be an organization like a temple."

"You're one hundred percent right, Kerm," said Kallen. "That's how I feel. If you can't trust the word of a temple, who can you trust?"

"All right, what can you do about it?"

"I'll tell you what I can do about it, Meyer," said Kallen, his tone determined. "I'm still a member of the board of directors. I could place it before the board and demand that they take action."

"So what would that get you? They'd take action, all right. They'd put it to a vote, and they'd vote Gorfinkle's way.

Remember, they've got a clear majority."

"Well, if the board should repudiate their solemn promises, I'd pick up my marbles and get out."

"And where would you go, Irv? To Lynn? To Salem? Where nobody knows you?"

"I'll tell you what I would do," Edelstein asserted. "I'd stay, but they'd whistle before they got a dime out of me."

Paff shook his head. "It wouldn't work, Doc. It might work in a church, but not in a temple. Our people don't ask for it; they demand it. It's part of the tradition. You know the old joke: The only thing two Jews can agree on is what a third should contribute to the support of the temple. No, if you were to give less than you gave last year, at the best everybody would think you had a bad year, that your practice was off. As for not giving at all — forget it. They just wouldn't let you get away with it; they'd bother you and pester you until you came across."

"Meyer's right," said Arons. "And you

know what it means? It means that from here on in, we'll be putting up the big money, we and our friends, and Gorfinkle and his gang will be spending it. They won't even do us the courtesy of consulting us about it."

"That's right," said Paff. "You don't think this new seating plan was brought up before the board, do you?"

"You mean it was just Ted Brennerman's idea? Dammit, they can't do that. A change like that has to be brought up before the board," said Kallen.

Paff shrugged his shoulders. "Oh, they'll bring it up at the meeting, just to make it legal, and they'll let us talk on it for a while, and then one of them will move the previous question and — zip — it'll go through like that." He snapped his fingers. "And that's how it's going to be from here on in. Make up your mind to it."

"And that's how they'll work this Social Action Fund. They'll appropriate all kinds of money, and they'll disburse it any way they want to. We'll give it, and they'll spend it."

"Aw, come on," said Kallen. "How much of a fund will they set up? Five hundred? A grand? So what? I remember my old man told me that years ago, in all the *shuls,* they had a fund that the president used to control and to disburse when, say, some poor guy would come to town and didn't have a place to sleep or needed a meal —"

"But that was charity," said Paff. "This money is to be used for politics. And it isn't the amount; it's the principle of the thing."

"All right, they won this election, and they're in power. So next year we work a little harder, and we take it away from them."

"Don't kid yourself," said Paff. "They're in, and they're in to stay. They got a different attitude toward this whole business than we have. They look at the temple organization as a corporation — which it is, of course, legally. When Wasserman was president and Becker and even Mort Schwarz, they put men on the board because they were either doing a lot of work for the temple or they hoped they would. The idea was to get the best men. But Gorfinkle's crowd — most of them work for large corporations, administrators, executives — and they look at it like a business corporation where if you get the majority of the stock, you take over all the top jobs and you fill the board of directors with your own men. So from here on in, their nominating committee won't nominate anyone unless they're sure he'll see things their way."

"Well, I think the least we could do is make the most God-awful stink tomorrow at the board meeting," said Arons, "and hope that we'll rouse enough people to rally to our support —"

"We can't," said Paff in his deep bass rumble.

"Why not?"

"Because we don't have anything for people to rally to. What are we going to do? Ask them to support our right to retain our front seats? Be practical."

"Well —"

"Then maybe what'll happen tomorrow *will* give us a better reason," said Kallen.

"And what's going to happen

tomorrow?'' asked Paff.

"Well, like I said, I was over at Nel Shaffer's last night. Nel and I are good friends, but mostly he hangs around with guys that are close to Gorfinkle, like Bill Jacobs and Hymie Stern. I got the impression from things Nel let drop that Gorfinkle was planning to announce the new committees tomorrow, and some of his appointments might be pretty raw from our point of view and from the point of view of a lot of members of the congregation.''

"Like what?'' demanded Edelstein.

"Like making Roger Epstein chairman of the Ritual Committee for openers,'' said Kallen.

"He wouldn't dare!'' said Edelstein.

"Why wouldn't he dare? He's his best friend. The two families are so close they're —''

"But the Ritual Committee,'' insisted Edelstein. "The man doesn't know a word of Hebrew. If the rabbi didn't announce the page, he wouldn't know what prayer to say next. He'd never been in a temple before he came here. His folks were radicals, free thinkers. And his wife — she's Gentile.''

''When she was converted, she became Jewish,'' Paff reminded him. ''That's the law. But that's a can of worms we don't have to open. If Gorfinkle appoints Epstein, it's still a raw deal against the congregation. And I'm not saying that because it's me he's going to replace.''

''All right,'' said Arons, ''so as soon as he announces it, we make a stink.''

''No.'' Paff was emphatic. ''I got an idea. When Gorfinkle announces his committees at the meeting tomorrow, we don't say a damn word. We sit tight.''

Everyone looked at him. ''And what does that get us?''

''Just trust me. I tell you I got an idea. Sorry, boys, but I can't give it to you now. Let's just see what happens tomorrow and follow my lead. If I don't say anything, don't you say anything.'' He looked around the table. ''Have I ever let you down?''

# 12

"But why the Ritual Committee?" asked Roger Epstein.

The Gorfinkles made a point of seeing their good friends, the Epsteins, at least once a week, usually on a Saturday night. They would go to a movie together or have an evening of bridge or sometimes merely sit around and talk, as on this Saturday night. Roger Epstein had waited until the women had gone into the kitchen before speaking.

"What's the problem, Roger?" asked Ben Gorfinkle.

Well, you know my background. What if the rabbi should raise an objection?"

Gorfinkle chuckled. "How can he when he won't even be at the meeting tomorrow?"

Epstein was a short, pudgy man, balding but with a tuft of hair in front, which he had a habit of pulling when disturbed. He pulled at it now. "So what? So he'll question it when he gets back. And he'll be right."

"He'll be wrong," said Gorfinkle flatly. "Appointment of committees and committee chairmen is purely an administrative function of the president."

"But this is the Ritual Committee. They supervise the order of the services. That makes it a concern of the rabbi, I would think. And what do I know about ritual? Besides, there's Samantha —"

"Look, Roger, you think you're required to be some sort of expert? You think Paff when he had the job was a specialist of the ritual? That's what the rabbi is there for. The way I see it, the Ritual Committee stands in relation to the congregation the way the School Committee here in town does to the citizens. You don't have to be a teacher or an educator to serve on the School Committee. We've got a superintendent of schools and principals and teachers for that. What you want on the School Committee is just somebody with common sense who has the welfare of all of us first and foremost in mind. Well, it's the same way with the Ritual Committee. There is a set order of prayers and it's shown in the prayer book. In case of any special question, there's the rabbi. As for the rest, I'd say that describes you to a T."

Epstein was still not convinced. "But why me?"

"Well, for one thing, the Ritual Committee parcels out the honors for the services, and especially for the holidays — that can be mighty important — and I want a man I can trust to head it up. For another thing, you're an artist —"

"Commercial artist," said Epstein with a deprecatory wave of the hand.

"An artist," his friend insisted. "There's a certain pageantry involved in religious services, and it takes an artist to sense it and bring it out."

"Well —"

From the kitchen, Samantha called out, "Coffee will be ready in a minute, boys," She came to the door. "How about some English muffins?" She was a good two inches taller than her husband; blonde and blue-eyed, with wide cheekbones, she looked like the daughter of a Viking.

"Just coffee for me, Sam," said her husband. "Too many calories."

"Aw c'mon, lover. You can indulge tonight. You've been a good boy all week."

"Well, all right. You twisted my arm."

"You'll have some, Ben, won't you?"

"You bet."

From upstairs, their daughter, Didi, called down. "You making coffee, Mum?"

A moment later she entered the room and waved to her parents' guests. She was a slim, elfin girl, whose hair was parted in the middle in two braids.

"You been here all evening?" asked Gorfinkle. "What have you been doing?"

"Telephoning, of course," her mother answered for her.

"Oh, Mummy," she protested, then

turned to the Gorfinkles. "We're getting up a cookout on the beach for Monday evening. When's Stu coming home?"

"Probably around noon Sunday," said Gorfinkle.

"Gee, I hope he hasn't made any plans. We're having all the kids who'll be coming home from school. I guess whoever is coming will be home by tomorrow. That's why we figured on Monday."

"Where are you having it, dear?" asked her mother.

"Over on Tarlow's Point."

"Monday — that doesn't give you much time to prepare. Have you called everybody?"

"Some. Bill Jacobs, Sue Arons, Adam Sussman. But, then, a lot won't be in until late tonight or sometime tomorrow. The chances are I'll see most of them over at the rabbi's house tomorrow afternoon."

"Why?" asked Gorfinkle. "Is he holding some kind of a meeting?"

"Oh, all the kids from the post-confirmation class sort of drop in the first Sunday they get back for vacation. You know, it's like an open house. They just talk, tell how things are going at school."

"Hm — that's interesting." Gorfinkle *was* interested. "How come? I mean, how did this — this tradition start?"

"No tradition. Just that sometimes he held the confirmation class at his house, and we kind of got into the habit of going there — you know, every now and then."

"And he's popular with you kids? You all like him?"

She considered. The question struck her as requiring thought, not because she was unsure of her feelings, but because they were hard to frame in words. "He's not fun, exactly," she said tentatively, "and he doesn't try to be pally or even friendly. He doesn't try to be anything, I don't think, but —"

"Yes?"

"An equal, I guess," she said, finally finding the words. "When you're with him, you don't feel like a kid."

# 13

The rabbi phoned Wasserman as soon as he arrived home Sunday. He caught him just returning from the board meeting.

"Mr. Wasserman? Rabbi Small. I'm sorry I wasn't able to get back in time. They had arranged for a party for me at the college for Saturday night. I didn't know anything about it."

"*Nu,* it happens. If the party was for you, you had to go."

"Tell me, did anything happen at the meeting? Anything special?"

"Well, Gorfinkle announced the new committees, like I thought."

"Yes? And how are they?"

"Well, if he appointed they should do a job, I guess it's all right. After all, he didn't appoint idiots. But if what he wanted is to start a fight, the appointments are good for that, too."

"That bad, eh? And what did Paff say? Was he there?"

"Oh, he was there. And that's the only nice part of it, because he didn't say a word, not Paff, not Edelstein, not Kallen, none of them. So I guess they're giving in, and for a while we'll have a little peace. But how long it will keep up?"

But the rabbi was disturbed. "What do you mean, they didn't say a word? Did they have a chance to? Was there time for discussion?"

"Oh, time, there was plenty, but no objections, no discussion, not one word, I tell you."

The rabbi waited for Wasserman to say more, but nothing was forthcoming. "I don't like it," he said at last.

"Why not?" said Wasserman. "You remember I told you it was like a marriage. If an open break doesn't develop, it can be fixed up."

"Yes, but if they don't talk at all, if the husband insults the wife and she doesn't even bother to answer, then it can mean that she's already made up her mind and it doesn't make any difference anymore. It seems to me Paff should have reacted. And I don't like the fact the others remained silent too."

"You think they decided something already? Well, maybe. It's possible. After what happened Friday night at the Brotherhood service . . ."

# 14

"All right, Meyer," said Dr. Edelstein as Paff wove his way through the traffic. "We sat tight like you asked us to, and Gorfinkle went ahead and nominated Roger Epstein as chairman of the Ritual Committee and Ted Brennerman as Chairman of the Seating Committee. After his talk Friday night, that was really rubbing it in. So what's the big plan already?"

Right after the board meeting Paff had insisted he, Edelstein, Kallen, and Arons go for a ride in his car. "I promise to bring you back in half an hour, so you'll have plenty of time to drive on home for lunch. I got something to show you boys."

He put his foot on the brake and brought the car to a halt opposite Hillson

House. All through the ride he had kept silent, refusing to be drawn, his only response to their questions a self-satisfied smirk. Now he said, "This is it, boys."

They looked at one another questioningly and then at him. "This is what, Meyer? Have you gone crazy or something?"

He looked at Edelstein and then turned to the back, where Kallen and Arons were sitting. "What you're looking at, gentlemen, is the site for the new temple. Prime shore front property. You said you'd pull out, Irving, and I told you there was no place else to go. Okay" — his hand swept out to encompass all before them — "here's a place."

No one said anything, but Paff seemed not in the least fazed by their silence, which made his deep rumble sound all the more booming. "All of us, we've all kicked in with big hunks of dough to the temple. Am I, are we going to let a bunch of Johnny-come-latelies push us around and tell us they're taking over and we should go peddle our papers someplace else?"

"You mean you want to start a new

114

temple, here on the site of this old ark?" said Edelstein, finally managing to put what they all felt into words.

"I mean I want to use this old ark, as you put it, for the new temple. She's a hundred and fifty years old, but she's sound, because that's how they used to build in those days. Of course, it will cost some money to fix up —"

"Some money?" said Arons. "It'll cost a fortune."

"So what? I made my money too late to change my habits. My Laura is after me I should have my suits made to order. 'You've got it now; spend it.' But I can't. I can't get interested enough in clothes to bother. When I play poker, I play penny ante, and I notice that I get as much fun out of winning ninety cents as I would if it were ninety dollars. And Irving is just as sore at losing thirty-two cents."

"Thirty-seven cents."

"Right! Thirty-seven cents. See what I mean? None of us would ever think of gambling more than he could afford to lose, so it doesn't make any difference if it's pennies or dollars; we get the same kind of kick out of it. I used to trade my car every three or four years; now I trade every couple of years. Each time I come in to trade, Al Becker tries to get me to switch to a Lincoln. 'A man like you,' he says, 'should drive a big car.' What am I? A kid? A college boy? I got to ride around showing off in a big car to impress some dizzy little broad? For me, a car is just to get from one place to another, and I'm used to a small car. But the temple — that's something else. I helped build it. Jake Wasserman started it, but I was right there behind him plunking down hard cash when it was needed. So now when Gorfinkle and his boys steal the place out from under our noses, do we just sit quiet and keep handing over money to them so they can spend it the way they like? What are we, a bunch of lousy Arabs we should steal away in our tents? I say, let's give them a fight; let's give them some competition."

"But the money —"

"So what? If I'm not going to use my money for things I don't care about, and I'm not going to use it for things I do care

116

about, what am I going to use it for?"

"Just what do you have in mind?" asked Edelstein.

"They're asking eighty thousand —"

"Eighty thousand? For an old ark?"

"Shore front, Irv, shore front. And there's a nice piece of land across the street that's part of the deal. That would make a nice parking lot. Believe me, it's a good investment even for a businessman."

"You mean you want us to buy it outright, just like that, with our own money?"

"Us and a few others I got in mind. We form a corporation and buy the place. Then we sell it to the new temple organization — at cost — and take back notes for our money. In the meantime it's a tax deduction. When the temple organization raises the money, they pay us off, and not only are we in the clear, but we've done a fine thing." He lowered his voice confidentially. "I'll tell you, I was thinking of it originally as a business deal."

"You mean you were planning to put up another bowling alley here?"

"You bet. But not just a bowling alley. I was going to combine it with a restaurant, maybe a dine and dance place, maybe billiards instead of bowling — it's getting big these days. And then while we were talking last night, I got to thinking what happened the day before, Friday —"

"You mean Ted's speech?"

"Believe me, that was just the climax. All day, from one town to another I got nothing but grief. You know, one of those days. So when we were talking last night, I thought to myself, What do I need another business enterprise for? At my age? Then I began thinking about this place as a temple. Lots of temples nowadays are converted homes — and a lot of them not half so fancy as this, let me tell you. We could set in some beams and pull out most of the interior walls on the first floor. That could be the sanctuary, and it would seat a couple of hundred people easy. We'd have to put in a new heating system and maybe the plumbing. But that's all. Structurally, it's sound. And then all the rooms on the second floor and the third floor could be

118

used for a school."

"So you'd have an old ramshackle place," said Kallen, "with a bunch of little bedrooms you're going to try to make into classrooms and a sanctuary, which, no matter how you arrange it, will still look like a dining room and living room knocked together. Like that place in Salem that started with fifty members, and they've still got about fifty members. For the last ten years now they've been trying to raise money to build, and they still haven't been able to."

"That's right, Irv baby, but there's a difference. Ours would be a shore front property."

"So?"

"Let me show you." He led them down the path to the beach, talking all the while.

"So what do people join a temple for? Some, because maybe they want to be big shots, but the great majority, they don't want to be members of the board of directors. They know it costs money, that the members of the board are always being hit. Most of them just want a place to go for the High Holidays and a place where they can send their kids to a school. But once you get started, that isn't what keeps a temple going. The High Holidays are only three days in the year. And daily prayers — there isn't a temple in the entire area that can guarantee ten men for a minyan every single day of the year. As for Friday night services, how many are we drawing now? Fifty? Seventy-five? Now for all those things, our place would be big enough and more than big enough."

He stopped abruptly to let them fully take in the water view. "The thing that really pulls in the members are the facilities for the Bar Mitzvahs and the weddings — the parties, in other words. Now you just think of the vestry in our temple, which is all we have for parties. Compare that with what we can offer here in Hillson House." He led them to the sea wall. "Think of it during the summer when most weddings take place. Think of a patio out in front here with a view of the beach. Now you're going to have a wedding, and you're going to spend anywhere from three to ten thousand dollars, and your wife and daughter are determined that things are going to be just right. You may not care — You're just the guy that foots the bills. But they care. They take a look at the vestry in the basement in the present temple, and then they come down to us. We show them they can have their wedding in a beautiful old mansion facing the ocean, and if the weather is warm, they can hold it outside, out of doors. You know, as a matter of fact, that's the Orthodox way to have a wedding, outdoors under the stars. Which would get the nod, the old temple or our place? You can bet that they would come to us. And we could afford to be exclusive. We wouldn't take just anybody. They'd have to petition for membership, and we wouldn't act on them right away. And if you don't think that would get them . . ."

"And what if the same thing happens again, Meyer?" asked Dr. Edelstein. "What if after a while the new members begin to outnumber us and try to take over?"

"I've thought of that," said Paff. "And I figure we can prevent it easy enough. We limit the number of members on the board, and then we write into the constitution that the founding members are permanent members. No sweat, believe me. And I'll tell you something else: I don't care if we don't pull so many the first couple of years. I'm a little sick of these shoe clerks and insurance agents and commission salesmen we got running things. That Gorfinkle crowd, they're a bunch of small-time guys, and I'd just as soon have the temple made up of our kind of people, who you run an affair you don't have to take them by the throat to squeeze the price of a couple of tickets out of them."

"When can we take a look at the place inside?" asked Kallen, and Paff knew he had sold them.

"Now you're talking," he said jovially. "Did you see that coach house in the front? That's part of the property. There's a son of a bitch of an old Yankee living there who is like a kind of caretaker. He's got a key." He led the way to the coach house door and rang the bell. "I've got ideas for this place, too," Paff went on. "How about this for a bride's dressing room? Maybe connected with the main building by a kind of covered walk. Or maybe better, extra classrooms for the school? Or even a clubhouse with ping pong tables and some gym stuff for the kids?"

"I guess he isn't in," said Arons after they had waited for several minutes.

"Tell you what," said Paff, "I'll get the key from the broker, and we can meet here tomorrow night. How about half past eight?"

"Okay with me."

"Suits me."

"Okay by me, too," said Arons. "But look, Meyer, you had this idea last night, right?"

"Right."

"So tell me, why were you so anxious we shouldn't say anything at the meeting this morning. Seems to me that if we had put up a fight, we would've got a lot of guys —"

Paff shook his head decisively. "You've

got it wrong, Kerm. Years ago there was a little grocery store in Chelsea, where my mother, may she rest in peace, used to trade. It was run by two brothers, Moe and Abe Berg. Then they had a fight, and Abe moved out and started another store of his own down the street. But even though the new store was a couple of blocks nearer our house, my mother went right on trading with Moe. And carrying bundles that couple of blocks meant something. When my father, may he rest in peace, asked her why she didn't trade at the new store, she said, 'How can I? Everybody will think I'm going there because I think Moe was wrong and Abe was right. And I feel that Moe was right.' See, this way, we're not asking people to take sides. We're not asking them to decide who's right and who's wrong, because if they decide against us, they won't come over to us even if we offer them a better deal for their annual dues.''

"I'll go along with that," said Kallen. "But I think it would help us if we could pull over some of the better respected members of the community. Now if

Wasserman and Becker would come over —"

"Wasserman would never come over," said the doctor, shaking his head.

"I think I know what might bring him around," said Arons suddenly.

"Yeah?"

"If we got the rabbi to come over first."

They all looked at him and then turned to Paff. "I don't think the rabbi would come," said Paff. "And I'm not sure that we want him. He's pretty independent."

"He's popular with the kids," said Arons stubbornly. "They like him. And you know how kids are these days. They rule the roost. None of them really want to go to Hebrew school. Who can blame them? So if the rabbi were with us, and the kids liking him, their folks might come over, if only to make sure that the kids go to school."

"You've got a point," said Paff. "What bothers me is that I don't think I could sell him on the idea in the first place."

"I'll bet Wasserman could."

"But he wouldn't," said Paff. "Remember, you're trying to use the rabbi to sell Wasserman."

"How about Becker?" asked Kallen. "I'll bet he'd go along. And he'd try to sell the rabbi on the idea. Then if we got the rabbi, we could get Wasserman."

"Now that's an idea," said Paff. "Tell you what, I'll drop in on Becker tomorrow." He winked. "It's getting to be trading time. This time maybe I'll be interested in a Lincoln."

# 15

Miriam opened the door of the rabbi's study to say that Mr. Carter had come.

"Mr. Carter?"

"Yes, David, the carpenter. He's come to fix the window cords and put up the screens."

Mr. Carter, a big, raw-boned man, stood framed in the doorway, with his heavy kit of carpenter's tools in one big gnarled hand showing no drag on his broad shoulders, like a businessman carrying a light attaché case. A lock of black hair fell across a slanting forehead; his face had the deep leathery tan of a man who spent much of his time outdoors.

"I arranged with the missus to come this morning," he said, "but when I got here, the house was closed and there was nobody home. I don't have much time today, but I can get started, and I'll finish up tomorrow or Tuesday."

"We were delayed and got back only an hour ago." The rabbi frowned. "Frankly, Mr. Carter, I don't like the idea of you working on Sunday, on your Sabbath. It doesn't look right."

"Oh, it's not my Sabbath, Rabbi, and most of the folks in town know it. So don't bother about what they might be thinking —"

"What do you mean? Are you the town atheist?" the rabbi asked with a smile as he led him inside to the windows that needed repair.

"No, I'm no atheist. I don't go to church, but I'm no atheist. I keep the Sabbath, but it's yours I keep, not Sundays."

"Seventh-Day Adventist?"

"No, although I hold with a lot they believe in. I keep the Sabbath because that's the day the Lord told me to keep."

"How do you mean the Lord told you?"

"Well, it's hard to explain — I mean just how He told me. You see it wasn't words, but if you translate it into words, it would be something like, 'Raphael, after spending six days in making the universe and everything in it, I rested, and that was a good thing. And what is good for Me is good for you, because I made you in My image. I want you to work six days in every week and then rest on the seventh. That's the right proportion. And one is as important as the other.' "

The rabbi looked at him doubtfully, wondering if he were pulling his leg, but Carter's face was open and without guile.

"And when did this happen?" asked the rabbi carefully, not knowing what sort of person he was dealing with.

"You mean when did the Lord give me that particular command?"

"I mean when did He talk to you?"

The carpenter laughed. "Bless you, Rabbi, it happens right along — real frequent. Sometimes more than at other times. Sometimes almost every day maybe for a week. And then weeks go by, and I don't hear a thing. The first time I had a lapse like that, I got real worried. I tried to make contact and I prayed. I said, 'Is there something Your servant has done that offends You?' And I didn't get any answer that day, but the very next day, He spoke to me again, and this time He told me not to worry about not hearing from Him — that He wouldn't be talking to me unless He had something definite He wanted to tell me. And that if I didn't hear from Him, it meant everything was going along all right. And thinking it over afterward, I had to admit that all that time things had been going along nicely for me — no trouble, no problems, just kind of humdrum, you might say."

Carter had already begun, and he continued as he talked. He cleaned all the old putty out of the sash and then scooped a handful of putty from a tin and began to roll it in his hands. He straightened up, and the rabbi was startled to see that although his complexion was swarthy, his eyes were a clear, piercing blue.

"It was right after I was married. Me and the wife had just got back from our honeymoon to Niagara Falls, and we were visiting around — you know, her folks — aunts, uncles, she showing me off, so to speak — and to my aunts and uncles so's I could show her off. It was kind of expected in those days. Well, we were visiting her Aunt Dorset and Uncle Abner. That was over by Lynnfield they lived. And there were other people there — cousins and such. And suddenly while we were all sitting in the parlor talking and Aunt Dorset was passing around some fruit, I heard a voice saying, 'Stand upon thy feet, and I will speak to you.' So, I got up and heard a voice talking, and it told me the first chapter of Genesis.

"Now, the point is that in all my life I had never read the Bible, but when I came to that day at Aunt Dorset's, I could repeat that first chapter of Genesis almost word for word."

"And what did your wife — and the rest of the company say?"

"They told me that I just stood there and didn't talk to anyone for some minutes. They thought I was under some kind of spell, maybe like a cataleptic, and I guess there was even some discussion about going for a doctor."

"And then?"

"And then the same thing happened the next day. I was on a job and working when it happened, and I was told another chapter. And I got a chapter or so every single day until I went right through the Pentateuch."

"And then?"

Carter shook his head. "After that I would get messages only when I needed them." He cut off a length of cord and ran it through the sash weight.

"How do you mean, when you needed them?"

He ran the weight up and down a couple of times to see if the pulley was moving freely. "Well, Rabbi, take the time the town voted on fluoridation. I was bothered about that. Myself, I didn't think it was a good idea. I don't believe much in chemicals — I mean taking them into your body. But the doctor who was taking care of my wife while she was having our last baby, I got to talking to him about it, and he was all for it. So I had doubts, you might say. Him being a fine man and respected. And then I got a message, and I knew I had been right in the first place." He swung the window in and then turned around and faced the rabbi. "Look at me, Rabbi. I'm fifty-eight and never been what you might call really sick a day in my life. I've got all my teeth, and I don't wear glasses. That's because I live right. I don't eat meat, and I don't eat candy. I don't drink tea or coffee or tonic."

"Was the injunction against meat one of the instructions you received? That's not quite the same as the dietary laws in the Pentateuch."

"Well, it is and it ain't, Rabbi. He expects you to use your intelligence." He snapped the edging of the window in place and screwed it down. "Now it says 'Thou shalt not kill.' And it also says that you can't eat part of a live animal. So that would seem to exclude the eating of flesh. Now I know it also says the kinds of animals you can eat — those with a cloven hoof and that chew the cud, but I figure that's for the mass of people who haven't got the strength of their own convictions. It's a kind of sop — for those who still hankered after the fleshpots of Egypt.

Couldn't get it out of their systems, you might say. So He allowed them to eat certain kinds of animals. But you can see He'd like it better if they didn't eat any."

"I see."

"There was another time when I was really sort of perplexed, and I got a message from Him. That was the time my oldest boy —"

The rabbi asked how many children Mr. Carter had.

"I got five, three boys and two girls. Moses, he's my oldest. Maybe you heard of him. Moose Carter? They call him Moose, he's so big. He was quite a football player at the high school last year and year before. Last year they came that close to winning the state championship. My boy's picture was in the papers a lot. There was sixty-seven colleges, Rabbi, sixty-seven that was interested in having my boy go there."

The rabbi showed he was impressed. "Was he also a good student?"

"No, just a good football player. They sent people down to see him, some of them did. Coaches or scouts. And they offered all kinds of things. Why, one offered girls.''

"Girls?"

"That's right. He said that they had a lot of co-eds that were pretty and rich and just aching to marry a great big handsome football hero. Then he says, and he winks, 'Or, you don't have to marry them.' I ordered him from the house. I didn't want my boy to go to any college and certainly not that one. I wanted him to get a job and go to work. But he finally did take one of those offers — a college in Alabama. I was all for putting my foot down and forbidding him, but his mother was mighty set on his going."

"And how did it work out?"

The carpenter shook his head dolefully. "He was there till Christmas, till after the football season, then they dropped him. He had hurt his knee, so he wasn't any use to them anymore, and besides, he was doing poor in his studies. So he came home. He's been home three months now and hasn't done a decent week's work. He works a couple of nights a week in a bowling alley in Lynn, and every now and then he gets an odd job to do, and that gives him a little spending money. I guess my wife gives him a few dollars now and then. She favors him — him being the oldest.'' He shook his head. ''I've suggested to him that he come in with me and learn my trade, but he tells me there's no money in it, that all the money these days is in wheeling and dealing. Wants to be a promotor. I tell you, Rabbi, the college ruined that boy. If it weren't for my wife, I'd order him from the house.''

He straightened up and looked about the room. ''That's about all I have here, Rabbi. It took a little longer than I anticipated. I won't be able to finish today, but don't you worry. When I undertake a job, I finish it.''

''It's just as well,'' said Rabbi Small, watching him carefully replace the tools in his kit. ''I'm expecting a group of young people to be dropping over a little later in the afternoon.''

''I'll come by tomorrow or Tuesday, depending how my work goes.''

''Fine, Mr. Carter. Whenever you have the time.''

# 16

"So then he says, 'I'm going to pass out copies of the new committees. I'll ask you to take these sheets home with you so that you can study them at your leisure, and then at the next meeting three weeks hence we can vote intelligently on confirmation.' " Malcolm Marks had been unconsciously mimicking the president. Now he resumed his normal tone. "And he passes out these mimeographed sheets, and I'm watching Meyer Paff. He's got his on the table in front of him, and he's reading the lists, sliding his finger on the page down the list and kind of making noises in his throat like he's pronouncing the names. And then he gets to Roger Epstein's name as chairman of the Ritual Committee, and I thought he was going to have a heart attack."

"But why should he be so upset?" asked his wife. "He must have known that Ben Gorfinkle wasn't going to reappoint him."

Marks made no attempt to hide his impatience. "Of course not. But Roger Epstein, for God's sake!"

The telephone rang. "I'll take it," called their daughter Betty from another room. And a moment later, "It's for me."

"Well, what's wrong with Roger Epstein?"

"With Roger Epstein as a person, maybe nothing. In fact, he's a very idealistic type who carries the whole world on his shoulders. But this is the Ritual Committee. You take the Building Fund Committee or the Membership Committee or even the High Holy Day Seating Committee, which all are important committees. Okay, Roger's fine and dandy. But strictly speaking, for the Ritual you should have not only a real pious type, I mean one who don't work on Saturdays and eats strictly kosher, but somebody who knows all about the rules of ritual. He's got to be practically a rabbi, strictly speaking. All right, we don't have too many like that. Maybe Jake Wasserman, but off hand I can't think of anybody else to speak of."

"So if nobody can do it, what's wrong with Roger Epstein?"

"Well, it's not exactly that nobody can do it. The point I'm making is that if you haven't got the type person who should be chairman of Ritual, you got to at least get somebody who, on the surface at least, seems okay. Now, Meyer Paff, maybe he doesn't know so much, but he keeps a kosher house —"

"Pooh! That's only because his mother-in-law lives with them, and she wouldn't eat there if they didn't have two sets of dishes. He couldn't let her starve to death, could he?"

"That's what I'm saying. It don't matter if he really believes in it, so long as he does it. That's what I mean by on the surface."

"All right. So what happened?" his wife asked.

"What do you mean?"

"When Paff saw that Roger Epstein was made chairman of the Ritual Committee. What happened already? What did he do? What did he say?"

"Nothing!" said her husband triumphantly.

She looked at him in amazement. "So what's the big *shpiel?* What's the excitement?"

"Don't you see? Paff has been the big wheel in the temple ever since it was built. He's never been president, but he's always been a power behind the throne. So Friday night Ted Brennerman gives him a ribbing right out in public. And don't tell me that Gorfinkle didn't know what Ted was planning. And from what I hear — we were down in the vestry at the time, so we missed it — Paff catches Ted up in the sanctuary, and he really lays him out in lavender. That's round one." He rotated a hand. "Mezzo, mezzo. Call it a draw; Paff gave it to Ted a lot harder than Ted gave it to him, but on the other hand, only a few people heard Paff, and everybody heard Ted. Yeah, I guess you could call it a draw.

"All right, round two. Gorfinkle doesn't let it lay; he comes out fighting. He says like, 'Make your play, Paff. Go for your gun. I'm not afraid of you. And I'm proving it by appointing my friend Roger Epstein to be chairman of Ritual, which not only you used to be chairman of and which, moreover, is a very special job that I wouldn't normally appoint Epstein to on account of his background, but I'm doing it right now, the first chance I got after Friday, just to show you who's boss. So put up or shut up.' "

"So he shut up."

"Not Meyer Paff. He don't give up that easy, and he don't back away from a fight. He just gets on his bicycle and goes in for a little fancy footwork to keep out of the way of Gorfinkle's reach so he can save his strength for the next round. The talk after the meeting was that he would line up his gang and either try to take over the town or burn it down."

"What do you mean burn it down? You mean he'd burn the temple?"

"Of course not. That's what they call a figure of speech," he said loftily. Then he lowered his voice. "Some people I talked to said they wouldn't be surprised if he pulled out of the temple and started one of his own."

"Over appointing Roger Epstein head of the Ritual Committee?"

"That and other things," said Marks defensively. "This thing has been building a long time."

She looked at him. "So where does that leave you?"

"That's just it. I'm like betwixt and between. I was appointed by Schwarz, and I got another year to go on my term. Ben Gorfinkle and Roger Epstein and the rest I'm kind of friendly with, but on the other hand, I'm friendly with Meyer Paff's gang, too. After all, if God forbid somebody needed an operation, we'd call Doc Edelstein, wouldn't we? So I can go either way. And my guess is both sides will be pulling for my vote."

Their daughter, Betty, sauntered into the room. She was short like both her parents. Her long blond hair was parted on one side and hung straight down over her shoulders, although one strand was looped over her ear with a barette and pushed forward to partially conceal her left eye. Where the hair was parted, one could see a trace of dark hair, suggesting it was time for another color rinse. Her innocent dark eyes were made knowing with eye shadow and a thin line of darker coloring that edged the lids. Her breasts pushed aggressively against her sweater, and her little rump rotated suggestively as she walked.

Her mother looked up in automatic question.

"A bunch of the kids are having a cookout tomorrow evening, at Tarlow's Point," she explained. "That was Didi Epstein. She wanted to know if I could make the scene."

Mr. Marks shot a significant glance at his wife, but she appeared not to notice. "Did you say you would go, dear?"

"I guess so. She said Stu Gorfinkle would pick me up — around five tomorrow."

"Did Didi say who else was going to be there?" asked her mother.

"Sue Arons and Gladys Shulman and

Bill Jacobs and I think Adam Sussman — you know, the kids who have been away to college and are back for the vacation."

"It's a lovely idea," said her mother. "It'll be nice to see all your old friends again."

When she left the room, Mr. Marks said, "See, it's started already."

"What's started already?"

"Buttering us up. All the time she was in high school they never gave her a tumble — that Epstein girl and the Gorfinkle boy, they always acted as though she wasn't good enough for them."

"That's ridiculous. Didn't she go to Didi Epstein's for the after-prom breakfast last year?"

"Sure, the whole senior class was invited."

"Well, you're wrong. They started making up to her before that — when she was accepted at Connecticut College for Women. She got more brains in her little finger, let me tell you — and they know it. That Stu Gorfinkle was turned down by all the schools he applied to, and he had to go to his fallback, Mass State. And Didi ended up at an art school in Boston, for God's sake, and she was so sure she was going to Wellesley because her mother was an alma mater there. And that little Sussman pipsqueak. I remember his mother distinctly telling the girls at her table at a Sisterhood lunch that her son had applied to Harvard, Yale, and Columbia. So he ends up at a dinky little college out in Ohio that nobody ever heard of."

"All right, all right, but you mark my words —"

The telephone rang. "It's for you, Dad," Betty called out.

"Who is it?"

"Mr. Paff."

Mr. Marks favored his wife with a triumphant smirk and left the room to answer the phone.

# 17

Sunday night supper was usually a pickup meal in the Gorfinkle household, where dinner was served at midday. But with Stu home, Mrs. Gorfinkle felt guilty about not providing him with a hot meal. So when he came in and asked what was for supper, she answered, "How about some hamburgers? I've got buns and potato chips."

"Oh sure, anything."

"Why, I'd like hamburgers for a change," said his father. "And a Coke."

"I'll take milk," said Stu.

"Milk with hamburgers?" questioned Mr. Gorfinkle.

"You suddenly kosher since you became president of the temple?" Stu asked sarcastically.

"No, but in my own house I don't like

to see them eaten together."

"But in a restaurant you don't mind? That doesn't make sense to me," said his son.

Gorfinkle resented being challenged by his son, but he tried not to show it. "Tastes in food never make sense, Stu. That's just how I feel about it. Your mother never serves butter, for example, when she's serving meat. When I was a youngster, the thought of it turned my stomach. But I always expect butter for my bread when I'm eating in a restaurant."

He was even more annoyed when his wife brought a pitcher of milk to the table, and automatically — as always happened whenever he was angry or crossed — the corners of his mouth turned up in a frozen little smile that had no humor in it, as some of his subordinates at the plant had found to their cost.

"He's so thin," she said apologetically as she filled Stu's glass.

Gorfinkle looked away from her and said abruptly to his son, "Where were you all afternoon?"

"Oh, some of the kids dropped in to see the rabbi. He sort of expects it. I did it during Christmas vacation, too. It's a kind of open house."

"And what did he have to say?" He could not help adding, "I'm sure he didn't talk about the kashruth regulations."

"Oh no. We just talk about what we're doing at school. Didi Epstein kind of kidded him about what they were teaching her in art school — learning to make graven images, you know."

"That Didi," said Mrs. Gorfinkle. "I bet he thought she was fresh."

"I don't think so. He said he didn't mind as long as she doesn't worship them. So then she told him about this painting she's doing on Moses receiving the Law. And he said he'd like to see it. She promised to bring it over tomorrow." Stu chuckled. "He's a pretty free-minded guy. You should've heard him down at Binkerton at this party they gave for him."

"Oh?" his mother remarked.

"There was this Father Bennett who's head of the Newman Club — like the

Hillel Club but for Catholics. He came over while I was sitting with him, and the Rabbi kind of needled him about his religion. Very smooth, very cool. And then this priest comes right back and asks how he stands in the faith department. 'Do you believe?' So the rabbi kind of smiles and says, "I guess I'm just like you; sometimes I do and sometimes I don't. Pretty sharp."

"Well, I don't think that's the proper thing for a rabbi to say," said Mrs. Gorfinkle flatly.

"Why not?"

"Well, if he's a rabbi, it seems to me the least he could do is believe all the time."

"That's just exactly where you're wrong. Do you believe all the time? Does Dad?"

"Now, just a minute, just one minute," said his father sternly. "I don't, and I don't suppose your mother does, but, then, we're not rabbis. What your mother means is that as a rabbi, it's his duty to believe. I can see him talking that way with a priest when they're alone together.

149

After all, they're both in the same profession. But I certainly don't think he should have said it in front of you or any of the other young people who were there.''

''Why not?'' demanded Stuart.

''Because you're not old enough or mature enough to —''

''And this business that's happening right here in the temple, I suppose I'm not old enough or mature enough to understand that either?''

''And what's happening here in the temple?'' asked his father quietly.

''There's going to be a split,'' his son said hotly. ''That's what's happening.''

Gorfinkle's voice was tight, controlled. ''Did the rabbi say that? Did he say there was going to be a split?''

''No, not exactly — but he didn't seem surprised when Sue Arons asked him about it.''

''I see,'' said the elder Gorfinkle. ''And what did he say?''

''Well, if you must know,'' said Stuart belligerently, ''he said there was no reason for a split and that if one occurred, it would be as much the fault of one side as the other."

Gorfinkle drummed the table with his fingers. "I see. And did he indicate what his attitude would be in the event of this supposed — split?"

"Yeah. A plague on both your houses."

"A plague on —?"

"He didn't use those exact words, of course." Stu showed his exasperation with his father's literal-mindedness. "What he said was that if a split should take place, well, he wouldn't care to serve any longer."

The corners of Gorfinkle's mouth turned up now. "He shouldn't have said that, not to you kids."

Stu was aware that his father was angry, but he resented the implication that he and his friends were not concerned. "What do you mean, 'you kids'?"

"I mean that he was trying to influence you, and he has no right to."

"Isn't that what rabbis are supposed to do, influence people, especially kids?"

"There's legitimate influence, and there's influence that's strictly out of line," said his father. "When the rabbi gets up in the pulpit and explains about our religion and its traditions, that's legitimate. That's what he gets paid for. But the rabbi is not supposed to interfere in temple politics. If he prefers one side to another, he's supposed to keep it to himself. And when he urges his point of view on a bunch of kids who don't know what's involved, then he's out of line. And I think I'm just going to have a little conference with him and tell him so."

"Look here," said Stu, suddenly worried. "You can't do that."

"And why can't I?"

"Because he'll know it came from me."

"What do you suppose he told you for? If he didn't think it would get back to me — and to the other parents?"

"He did no such thing. He wouldn't, not the rabbi. He's straight."

"Straight? He's just a guy who's trying to keep a job."

Stu put down his half-eaten second bun and, pushing his chair back from the table, he rose, his face white with anger. "Yeah, you can go and wreck an

152

organization, and that's all right, an organization that's just a sideline with you, a hobby that makes you feel like a big shot. You don't even care about it enough to keep kosher or anything like that, but if someone whose whole life is involved in it tries to preserve it, then you got to rub him out."

"Finish your meal, Stu," pleaded his mother.

"Sit down," ordered his father. "You don't know what you're talking about."

But the young man flung away from the table.

"Where are you going, Stu?" his mother called after him.

"Out!"

A moment later they heard the outer door bang.

"Why do you always fight with him?" asked Mrs. Gorfinkle plaintively.

"Because he's an idiot." He, too, rose from the table.

"Where are you going?"

"To make some telephone calls."

But the phone rang just as he reached for it. It was Ted Brennerman on the other end. "Ben? Ted. I got it via the grapevine that Paff and his gang are beginning to line up people."

"You mean to vote against my appointments? Naturally —"

"No, Ben, not to try to outvote us — to pull out and start another temple."

"Where'd you get that from?"

"Malcolm Marks. Paff called him."

"And I just found out that the rabbi has been shooting off his mouth to the kids to have them bring pressure on their parents. I think I'm beginning to understand. Look, we've got to have a meeting on this, and tonight. You got a list of the board members? Well, you know which ones are with us a hundred percent. Start calling them. You take the ones from A to M, and I'll take the rest. We'll meet here at my house, say around ten o'clock. That'll give everybody plenty of time."

# 18

From the bureau drawer Moose Carter selected a pair of Argyle socks. Though it was Monday and nearly noon, he still wasn't dressed. He sat on the edge of the bed as he drew them on absentmindedly while contemplating the immediate problem — money. In the room next door his sister Sharon, he knew, was lying on her bed reading. She was always reading.

"Hey, Sharon," he called through the wall, "got any scratch?"

"No." He had not expected anything else, but it was worth a try. He leaned close to the wall and spoke with great urgency. "You see, I've got this job lined up. The guy's in town, in Boston —" He heard the squeak of her bed and then a door slam closed. She had gone out.

"Bitch," he muttered.

He raised the edge of the mattress to remove the gray flannel slacks he had placed between the box spring and mattress the night before. As he drew them on he considered the possibilities offered by his brother Peter's room. The kid had a paper route and always had money. He wouldn't lend a nickel, though. He thought more of money than of his skin. But he wasn't home now. On the other hand, the kid was good at hiding it, and if Sharon heard him moving around in his room, she'd rat on him. His shoulders gave an involuntary twitch as he remembered the last time he had been caught borrowing from Peter's hoard; his father had showed his disapproval — with a half-inch dowel rod.

Still debating with himself the chances of a quick foray into Peter's room, he selected a yellow shirt from his meager supply. He heard the downstairs door open and close, signaling the return of his mother from her shopping. Hell, she'll give it to me, he thought and quickly finished dressing. The black tie, already knotted, needed only a quick jerk to tighten. He squirmed into his sport jacket, and with the aid of a forefinger, worried his feet into his loafers. Then he hurried down the stairs.

She was in the kitchen putting away the groceries. "You going to see a girl?" she asked sourly, seeing the way he was dressed.

He grinned at her, a wide infectious grin. "Girls is for nighttime, Ma, you know that. I'm going into town."

"Town?"

"Yuh, Boston. I gotta chance for a job. It's a special deal. I might be late getting home."

"Your father doesn't like it if you're not at the table at dinnertime."

"Well, gee, sure, I know, Ma, but I'll be hitchhiking back."

"You mean you haven't even got bus fare back?"

"I only have a dime. That's the truth. I had to get some stuff at the store for a job that I was doing for old man Begg, and he forgot to pay me back, and I forgot to ask him."

"Didn't he pay you for the job either?"

"Oh no, he never pays me until Friday, the end of the week."

"And that Mr. Paff at the bowling alley?"

"He'll pay me tonight."

"And how does it look that a boy like you should be thumbing rides," she demanded. "Why don't you get yourself a regular job?"

"Carpenter like Pa? No thanks. I've been able to manage since I got back, haven't I? Once in a while a fellow gets strapped. Well, that can happen to anyone. Now if this deal that I'm working on comes through, I'll be all set."

"What kind of a deal?" she asked.

"Oh, it's kind of promotion work. This fellow I knew — I met him in school when I was in Alabama — he's coming up North and he's building up an organization."

"And you're going to see him without a penny in your pocket?"

"Well, I'm not going to *tell* him that I'm broke," he said tartly.

"He'll see it in your face. He'll read it in your eyes," she said. "Like I do." She fumbled in her apron pocket and took out a coin purse. "Here, here's two dollars. That's all I can let you have, but you'll be able to get the bus both ways." She held the crumpled bills out to him. "Now you make sure you get home in time for dinner."

"Well, gee, Ma. I mean, I might have some business to talk over. He might ask me to have dinner with him. I can't just break away and say I've got to get home, my folks expect me home for dinner."

"Well, if you find that you're going to be delayed, you call up. Just excuse yourself and say you have a previous engagement you've got to cancel, and you call up and say you're going to be late. Now that's the proper way to do it. And if this man is any kind of businessman, he'll respect you for it."

"Okay, Ma. Guess you're right. Thanks for the money. You'll get it back no later than Friday."

From the hall closet he took his light-beige cotton raincoat, turned up the collar, and surveyed himself in the hall mirror. He was satisfied at what he saw —

the young collegian, just like in *Playboy*. From the mirror he could see that his mother was watching him and that she was proud. He winked at his reflection and then with a gay, "Be seeing you," he left.

# 19

Didi cupped her hand over the mouthpiece of the telephone and whispered to her mother, "Remember that boy from school I told you about? Alan Jenkins? The colored boy? Well, he's in Lynn and wants to come over. What shall I tell him?"

"Ask him to come over, if you want," said Mrs. Epstein matter-of-factly. "Does he have a car?"

"He's got a motorcycle. But what about the cookout —"

"Invite him along if he wants to come."

"You think it will be all right."

"I don't see why not. What's he like, anyway?"

"Oh, he's a little older than most of the freshmen; he was out working a couple of years. He's terribly talented. And he's easygoing and pleasant — I mean he's not surly or — you know — angry like some of them. I mean at school, it being an art school, well, it doesn't make any difference. I mean we don't think of him as being different, if you know what I mean."

"Then —" Mrs. Epstein shrugged her shoulders.

Didi uncupped the mouthpiece and said, "Oh, Alan? Sorry to keep you waiting. Look, some of the kids I went to school with — we're having a cookout on the beach. How would you like to make the scene? . . . About six or eight of us. . . . You can? Good — Oh, I just thought of something; I promised our rabbi I'd show him that painting I was working on at school — you know, Moses and the tables of the Law? So why don't you pick me up there? . . . No, we won't get hung up. . . . All right, here's what you do: Take the shore road out of Lynn and go along until the first set of traffic lights. . . ."

Alan gunned the motor and then let it

die. Didi in white slacks climbed down from behind him, and he walked the bike up the driveway to the garage. "That rabbi seemed like a straight guy," he said. "Funny, I thought he'd be an old crock with a long beard. I thought all rabbis have beards."

Didi giggled. "No, just the kids at school. Come to think of it, I've never seen one with a beard."

"I figured he'd talk like a preacher — you know, about God and all that."

"Rabbis really aren't preachers; they're more like teachers," she explained. "Actually, according to our rabbi, his real job is interpreting and applying the law — like a lawyer or a judge."

Mrs. Epstein greeted them in the living room. "Your first time in Barnard's Crossing, Mr. Jenkins? Didi has told me so much about you." He was a nice-looking young man, of a deep coffee-brown. His lips, though bluish, were not over-large. His nose, too, was high-bridged and well-formed. His hair was cut close to his head, and she was pleased to see no attempt had been made either to straighten or to smooth it down. He was of medium height but had a large chest and square shoulders, which seemed tensed at the moment.

"Yes, ma'am. I've been to the North Shore a couple of times — to Lynn. There's a guy — a man who sometimes sells some of my paintings for me there —"

"An art dealer? I didn't know there was an art store or gallery in Lynn," she said, offering him a chair.

"No, ma'am. He's got like a bookstore and greeting cards and some gift items — things like that. He hangs up some of my paintings when he's got the space, and when he sells one, he pays me."

"And do you sell many?" she asked.

He laughed, a fine, open laugh. "Not enough to retire on. I'm riding down to New York first thing tomorrow morning, and I was hoping he might have some loot for me." He shook his head. "Zilch — although he did say he had a couple of people interested in one picture."

"And what kind of pictures do you paint, Mr. Jenkins?"

"Oh, Alan does these marvelous abstracts —"

An auto horn sounded outside. "There's Stu now. Come on, Alan," said Didi.

"Take a sweater, dear. It can get chilly on the Point."

"Don't need one."

"Well, have a nice time, dear. Goodbye, Mr. Jenkins. And good luck on those paintings."

# 20

As Moose found himself picking his way between clumps of trash barrels and groups of squalling children, who spilled all over the street in the South End of Boston, he began to have misgivings. To be sure, the street must at one time have been very fine; it was divided in the middle by a broad grass plot, with wooden park benches set at regular intervals. But the grass even this early in the spring looked ill-cared for, and a litter of papers, tin cans, and bottles had piled up under the benches. Once grand brownstone-front town houses with short flights of granite stairs, each with its wrought-iron railing, were set back from the sidewalk. The ornate wooden doors, which no doubt had had massive brass knockers and brass doorknobs, showed years of wear and

166

abuse; there was a hole in the door where the knocker had originally been, and instead of the doorknob only a round hole with a thong of greasy leather hanging from it to serve the purpose. Peeling, blistered paint showed layers of different colors on the door, flanking which were long, narrow windows suggesting high-ceilinged rooms inside. But most of the windows were cracked, and in one case the window had been shattered and replaced by a piece of weatherbeaten plywood. The sidewalks and sides of the houses were liberally sprinkled with chalk graffiti.

Moose found the number he was looking for and climbed the stairs. Finding no bell button (there was only a hole through which a couple of wires protruded), he rapped on the door. He waited a moment and, receiving no answer, pushed the door open. It was held closed by a coiled spring under considerable tension, so that the moment he released it the door slammed shut. At the noise a slatternly old woman poked her head into the vestibule and looked at him inquiringly.

"I'm looking for Mr. Wilcox," said Moose.

"Top floor, last bell," she said and closed her door.

Then Moose noticed a row of mailboxes, and he pushed the button under the name. Almost immediately there was an answering "Hello" through the speaking tube.

"I'm Moose Carter, Mr. Wilcox," he called into the tube. "I spoke to you on the phone."

"Come on up."

His initial misgivings were immediately allayed as he stepped inside. The room was large and well-furnished. There was an Oriental rug on the floor and oil paintings in heavy gold frames on the walls; large overstuffed chairs were scattered around the room, and facing a large window, from which could be seen the neighboring rooftops, was a massive sofa. Nearby was a marble-topped desk in carved mahogany and behind it a black-leather modern swivel chair set on a chrome pedestal.

Wilcox himself was not what Moose had expected. With his flannel slacks and tweed jacket, he reminded him of a youngish professor, like some of the ones he had known in college. His brown hair was cut close and showed signs of graying at the temples; his manner, easy and friendly.

"Some view you've got here," said Moose, approaching the window.

"I like it," said Wilcox. "I like to sit on that sofa there and just look out over the rooftops. Very relaxing."

"It's nice," said Moose. "I wouldn't have . . ." He stopped.

"Expected it? You mean from the appearance of the street? A lot of these houses are being bought and fixed up, like this one." He smiled, and it was a nice smile. "It's a sort of private slum reclamation project. This apartment here belonged to an artist friend of mine. He took a long-term lease and fixed it up as a studio, which accounts for the picture window. Then he decided to go to Europe. It's actually in a convenient part of the city here."

"This your office, Mr. Wilcox?"

The other eyed him speculatively and then said, "I do some business here." He motioned Moose to the sofa and then sat down at the other end, facing him. "You said you were interested in working with us."

"That's right, sir."

"Well, the stuff we deal in is not hard to get in the city, and there are plenty of people, retailers, who buy the stuff on their own from Tom, Dick, or Harry, and I guess maybe they make out all right. But we don't operate that way. We're an organization. Maybe at first it looks as though it might cost you a little bit more, but our people think it's worth it. When you buy from us, you can be sure the stuff is good. You don't have to worry whether it's mixed with oregano or catnip or worse, which could get you into a lot of trouble. You get any customers for other kinds of stuff we can supply them, but when we sell grass, grass is what you get. That's the way I like to operate.

"There are advantages to working with an organization," Wilcox went on. "We keep the competition down. Somebody comes in town and gets a supply, passes it on to his friends, or maybe sells it at his cost, we don't bother with that. But someone coming into your territory who is an operator, well — we take care of it. And then there are times when you get into trouble, and if it can be fixed, we'll fix it. Of course, one reason we'd like to have you with us is that the kids all know you and you can operate on a friendly basis with customers in your hometown, and that's a good thing."

Moose hesitated. "How about —"

Wilcox nodded. "Yes, the territory has been assigned already, but we're not entirely satisfied with the way it's been operated. Then you can argue that the territory has grown too big for one man." He reflected. "Maybe that would be the best angle. You need two to really work a good territory. So you can go and see him and tell him we said you're to come in with him. The arrangement will be a straight fifty-fifty split. Of course, he's paid for his present stock, so you could offer to work that off on a commission or a percentage basis. Say a quarter. I'd say that would be about right. A quarter on the old stock and a half on the new. We'll see how that goes for a while, and then maybe we'll make some changes.''

''What kind of changes?''

Wilcox pursed his lips. ''Well, if things go the way I'm hoping, there's no reason you couldn't handle it yourself some day. So we'd transfer him — that's right, we'd transfer him to another territory. That's kind of our regular policy. We transfer him to another territory.'' Wilcox opened a cigarette box on the coffee table and offered Moose a cigarette.

''When would I start?'' asked Moose, lighting up.

''What's wrong with right away? Tomorrow, day after, tonight if you can arrange it.''

''Well, when will you talk to him? I mean when are you going to let him know?''

Wilcox smiled. ''I figured on you telling him.''

''Me? But — but what if he doesn't believe me?''

"Well, I was counting on you to make him believe you. You might consider it a kind of test. Yes, that's what it is — a kind of test. You take an operation like ours, we don't have too much staff. Every man operates on his own. We can't have a man calling up the home office every time he runs into a little problem. So — you've got your instructions; you look like a persuasive lad" — he eyed Moose's size and smiled — "you'll know what to do. Of course, if he does contact us, we'll tell him what the situation is."

"Oh, sure, Mr. Wilcox, I understand. And I'd like you to know that I appreciate this chance, and I'll do my best —"

Wilcox smiled sardonically.

"I mean it, sir. I —"

Wilcox cut him off with a wave of the hand. "Everybody tries to knock a little off the top. We expect it. Just don't get greedy." He reached for his wallet. "You need a little expense money to tide you over?"

"I can manage."

Wilcox riffled through a sheaf of bills and then drew out two new twenties.

"Well, call it an advance. Just a minute." He left the room but returned almost immediately with a plastic tobacco pouch, which he tossed to Moose. "There's an ounce package. You can consider this a kind of promotion package, uh — samples. There's no charge for this. But after this, everything is cash on the barrelhead. Get it?"

"Oh sure. And thanks."

Wilcox went over to the cigarette box and pressed a catch on the side. The top tray of cigarettes swiveled to one side, exposing another layer of cigarettes underneath — somewhat irregular in shape and obviously homemade. "Have a couple for yourself," he offered.

"Gee, that's neat."

Wilcox smiled. "A gimmick. Nothing to rely on if cops get around to actually looking." Moose picked up a cigarette from the box, rolled it in his fingers, and sniffed deeply.

"I don't think you'd better smoke it here. Take a few with you. You got a cigarette case? Wait a minute." He searched in the desk drawer and brought out a flat cigarette case of German silver. He slid a number of the cigarettes inside the elastic band of the case. "Here," he said. As Moose reached for it he had another thought. From the top tray of the cigarette box he took several ordinary cigarettes and slid them alongside the others. "Now you got an assortment," he said.

# 21

Much of the beach was rocky, and what sand there was was coarse and gravelly. But it was secluded. Principally that was because it was situated on a kind of peninsula, and when the tide was in — which would be shortly — it was surrounded by water on three sides. Broken branches from the stand of pines provided plenty of wood for a fire; and driftwood was plentiful, too, since the point jutted out into the current.

Bill Jacobs, who had been a camp counselor for the last two years, took command automatically. "Someone, put the beer and Cokes in the water to chill. You guys get some of these bigger rocks for a fireplace, and the chicks can gather the wood."

"Hey," said Adam Sussman, "remember

when we had a cookout here some years ago — the Sea Scouts? Were you in that, Stu?"

"Yeah, I remember. There was some kind of stink about the fire. The beach isn't public; it belongs to the Hillson estate. We didn't have a permit, that was it. Say, Didi, did you get a permit for a fire tonight?"

"We don't need one," said Didi, suddenly apprehensive. "I'm sure we don't. That's only during the summer."

"Well, all they can do is kick us off, I suppose." said Stu philosophically. And then he laughed, and Didi saw she was being ribbed and chucked a handful of sand at him. "You really had me going there — permit for a fire!"

"Well, let's at least wait until it gets dark," said Sue Arons. "That's when a fire is fun."

Everyone scattered to carry out his assigned task. Bill arranged the large rocks in a circle for the fireplace, and after the boys had finished, they helped the girls gather wood. After a while there was a big enough pile for Bill to call a halt. "Okay, you guys, I think we've got enough."

"I could use a beer right now," said Adam.

"Yeah, me too," said Stu. He looked at his watch. "Damn, I've got to cut out around six thirty to drive my folks over to Lynn."

"But we'll be doing our cooking around then," protested Didi. "You'll miss all the food."

"It was the only way I could get the car," he said. "But I'll be back in no time. Say, who's got the beer?"

"When are you going to light the fire, Bill?"

"I don't know. After it gets dark and we start getting hungry. Anyone in a hurry?"

"No, let's wait a little while."

The sea was calm, almost unnaturally so. They could hear the gentle swish of the waves as they struck against the sea wall. From the distance came the screeching of sea gulls. Otherwise the air was still, and there was something about the quiet that tended to restrict conversation. They had paired off now, and what talk there was tended to be between couples, and they kept their voices low. They sipped their drinks reflectively and waited for it to grow dark.

Adam Sussman rested his head on his girl's lap; encouraged by his example, the others began to maneuver into more intimate positions. Suddenly Sussman sat up and exclaimed in disgust, "Jee-sus."

"What's the matter?"

"We got company." He pointed at a lone figure coming toward them.

"Hey, it's Moose Carter," said Stu.

"God's gift to women," said Didi.

"Hiya, Moose." Bill Jacobs waved lazily at him.

"Hi, kids. H'lo Bill, Stuie. And Didi and little Sue. Betty baby, where you been?" Then he saw Jenkins. "Why shut my mouf if we haven't got us a genuwine integrated cookout."

"Take a can of beer and cool it," said Bill Jacobs shortly.

"Sho, sho, as we say down in Alabam. Don't mind if I do." He ripped open the top of a beer can and said, "Any of you ever seen this before?" He threw his head back and let the beer gurgle down his throat without a ripple of his Adam's apple.

"Alan Jenkins. Moose Carter."

Neither man offered his hand, but both said "Hi."

"Have another," suggested Jacobs.

"I guess I can use one. Maybe I'll sit down for this one." As he saw Stu move over to make room for him near Jenkins, he said, "I'll just sit over here with my old sweetheart Betty — in the front of the bus, if you don't mind, Stu."

Didi felt Stu's hand clench under hers. She peered at her watch. "It's half past six. If you have to go for your folks, you'd better leave now."

"Maybe I better stick around for a while," he muttered.

"No, go now," she whispered back. "It'll be all right."

It was only after Stu had been gone for some minutes that they felt the first drops of rain.

# 22

When it was his turn to lecture the executive trainees on personnel management, Ben Gorfinkle always ended with a short disquisition on the recalcitrant subordinate.

*In dealing with a subordinate who has got out of line, even if you hold all the trumps and can fire him like that — a snap of the fingers — it's better to first give him a chance to shape up. Because if he's a good man and shapes up, then you're all set. But if you fire him, you have to get a replacement. And how do you know he won't be just as bad? It's a good idea to arrange for a conference.*

As soon as he got home from the plant Monday, he called the rabbi. "I'd like to get together with you, Rabbi, for a little conference. We really haven't talked face to face since I became president, and I think there are a lot of things we ought to iron out.''

''Any time at all.''

*Sometimes it's a good idea to arrange for the conference well in advance so that he can stew for a while. Other times, you may find it better to hold it right away, with no prior notice, so that he's kind of taken by surprise and is unprepared. It depends on the circumstances.*

''How about this evening?''

''I go to the minyan at seven.''

''I've got a dinner engagement at that time, but if we could get together a little before —''

''That would be all right.''

''Stu has my car —''

''I can come over to your house,'' said the rabbi.

As the rabbi shook hands with Gorfinkle he could not help thinking that with each of the presidents of the temple, his relations had been different. With Jacob Wasserman, the first president who had originally selected him, there had been not only mutual respect, but a true friendship. In spite of the difference in their ages, they liked each other as people, and that first year at Barnard's Crossing the Wassermans had had them to dinner on any number of occasions, and the Smalls felt themselves free to drop in on them on a Sunday afternoon for a cup of tea and talk. He had needed a friend in the president then. Looking back, he realized that he had been incredibly young and inexperienced and that only the strong friendship of Wasserman and the respect with which the old man was held by the entire community had saved him from countless embarrassments, including the ultimate embarrassment of not having his contract renewed after his trial year.

With Al Becker, who had taken over after Wasserman, his relations were quite different. Originally Becker had been the leader of the opposition, and only by the sheer luck of being able to help him in a personal matter had the rabbi been able to win him over. Becker had felt guilty about his original opposition and became not only respectful but at times almost obsequious. Now he had no stauncher champion than Becker, but he never felt quite at ease with him.

Morton Schwarz, the third president and Gorfinkle's predecessor, had no such attitude toward the rabbi. He was friendly and sometimes even unbent enough to josh him about his little shortcomings, such as his chronic tardiness and his tendency to forget appointments that he didn't care to keep in the first place. But in Schwarz's mind, at least, this was strictly a one-way street, and when the rabbi occasionally answered in kind, he was sure he was considered presumptuous. However, he had grown in the years that he had been at Barnard's Crossing, and he had found the president's attitude amusing rather than annoying. The fact that he had been given a five-year contract may have had something to do with it.

Ben Gorfinkle was something else again. He knew something of his capacity from having sat on the board with him for several years, but he had had little chance to work with him. What few dealings they had had to date had been quite neutral, neither friendly nor hostile.

*Start by putting him at ease. Establish a friendly atmosphere.*

Gorfinkle led the way into the living room, and when they were both seated, he said, "You quite comfortable there, Rabbi? Would you prefer this chair?"

"No, this is fine."

*Encourage discussion, but keep him on the defensive.*

He smiled benignly. "I wish you'd tell me, Rabbi, what your idea is of the purpose and function of a temple and what you consider the rabbi's responsibility to the institution."

The rabbi recognized the gambit and declined it. He smiled. "I've spent the last half dozen years doing just that. Surely you didn't call me — so urgently and under pressure of a pending engagement — to hear me synopsize what I've been saying ever since I came here. I'm sure you have something to say to me."

Gorfinkle nodded in appreciation. He was silent for a minute and then he said, "You know, Rabbi, I don't think you understand what the temple is all about. I'm not sure that any rabbi ever does.

185

They're too much involved in it; they have a professional interest.''

"Indeed! Perhaps you can explain it to me.''

*In your part of the discussion, appear frank and open. Let him feel that you are not trying to conceal anything.*

Gorfinkle disregarded the rabbi's irony. "You think of a temple as being started by a group of religious men, which once underway, draws other religious-minded people.'' He shook his head. "Maybe there's one man who is really religious, like perhaps Wasserman, but the rest are interested in it merely as an organization. And once the organization is successful — and it takes a lot of work — then the original group becomes a drag on the organization, and a different type of person has to take over. Sometimes originators get so puffed up with their success that there's no living with them. They act as though they own the place because they started it. It rubs the new people the wrong way. That's what happened here, and in a sense, that's how I happen to be president. But it goes even deeper than that: To start an enterprise calls for a different set of talents than those you need to keep it going. They're two kinds of people."

"They're both Jews," the rabbi observed.

"That's only incidental, Rabbi."

"Incidental? In a synagogue?"

Gorfinkle nodded. "That's right. You're aware that there are two factions in the temple, mine and the one led by Meyer Paff. Now Paff, for all his Orthodoxy, isn't terribly concerned about Judaism or religion in general. All these people who are involved with the temple, men and women both, do you think it's because they're religious? Or that religion is important to them?" He shook his head in violent negation. "No, Rabbi. Do you know what they're interested in? They're interested in the temple as an organization.

"Every man wants to be something, to be somebody. He wants a sense of achievement, of accomplishment. He's gone to school, and he's gone to college, and he dreamed of being somebody, of being important. Then he got himself a

187

job or established a small business of some kind and thought at last he was on the road. And now at the age of thirty-five he realizes that he's not going to become the President of the United States or lead an army; he's not going to win a Nobel Prize; his wife is not a movie actress, and his children are not geniuses. He begins to realize that the business of getting up in the morning and going to work and coming home to go to sleep in order to get up in the morning to go to work — that is not going to change in any dramatic fashion. His whole life is going to be pretty much like that until he dies. And when he dies, his family will remember him, and that's all.

"That's a hard thing to swallow in a society like ours, where everybody starts out with the assumption that he can be President of the United States or at least a millionare. So these people throw themselves into organization work so they can be somebody. It used to be lodges where they could wear a fancy uniform and have a fancy title. Well, lodges are a little out of fashion these days, and in a

Yankee town like Barnard's Crossing it's not easy for newcomers, Jew or Gentile but especially Jewish newcomers, to have very much to do with the politics of the town. But here the temple is an organization that is theirs. They can do something and be somebody. There's the temple and the Brotherhood, and for the women there is the Sisterhood and Hadassah. All they have to do is do a little work, and sooner or later they become a somebody. They become chairman of a committee, or they become an officer. They get their names in the papers. And if you don't think that's important, you talk to some woman who folded napkins, say, for the Hadassah luncheon and didn't get her name mentioned along with the rest of the committee that was involved in setting it up.

"But to get back to Paff. All the time he was running things he was important. Now that he isn't running things, he's not important, and it irks him."

"If it were only that," said the rabbi mildly, "would he have contributed such large sums and done so much work and given so much time?"

Gorfinkle shrugged his shoulders. "What is a large sum to you, Rabbi, is not a large sum to Meyer Paff. You grow up to a certain standard of living. When you come into a lot of money, do you think you can change that standard very radically? You buy a bigger car, you buy an extra suit or two, and you pay a little more for it; you have a few extra pairs of shoes, and you pay a little more money for them. It's still nothing. There's this vast sum of money coming in, and you're nowhere near being able to spend it. So what do you do with it? You use it for advertising. You move out of your thirty-thousand-dollar house into a hundred-thousand-dollar mansion. You buy paintings; you get an interior decorator. Why? Because you suddenly developed artistic sensibilities? No. You're successful, but you don't feel any different. So you do the things that prove to other people that you're successful. Their envy or respect make you feel like somebody. Some go in for display, and some let themselves be seen with expensive-looking women. Others, like Paff, give their money to various worthwhile institutions."

"And you?" asked the rabbi.

*If challenged, don't hesitate to admit your own shortcomings. It makes for a better atmosphere.*

Gorfinkle shrugged. "I'll admit it. I'm no different." He grinned. "You might even say I'm a classic example. I'm an electronics engineer. When I got through at MIT, the field was comparatively new at the time. I graduated high in my class, and I figured I'd be heading up a big electronics lab by the time I was thirty. But there was the war, for one thing, and that delayed me. Then when I did get started, I found that the promotions didn't always go to the most able man — not in big corporate industry, anyway. Being a Jew didn't help either. And then the Ph.D.'s began to appear on the scene — overeducated nincompoops. That didn't help the picture. So what do you do? If you're a married man with a child, you can't go back to school. You shift to another job that looks as though it might lead somewhere. And it doesn't, of course. You try again, and it doesn't pan out either. I even switched to a small outfit where there was talk about stock options — talk — but there would be a chance to grow with the company, and the company looked as though it might grow. I even took a small cut in salary, because I figured this was my last chance. In this business, you've got to make it when you're still in your thirties or you don't make it at all.

"For a while it looked good. And then we sold out to a big outfit, one of the giants, and I was working for a big corporation again. So now, when I'm forty-five, I'm a section head, which means I'm middle management. And that's what I'll probably be until I retire. I admit that when I first threw myself into temple politics, it was because I felt I could do a better job. I still think that's part of it. But I don't kid myself. I know that a good part of it is just to be somebody, to have an influence on the people around me."

"Aren't you being overcynical and missing the main point, as cynicism usually does?" the rabbi asked.

"How do you mean?"

"Well, you say that some do it by building big houses or other kinds of ostentation, while still others do it by contributing to good causes. That's the major difference between people, isn't it? Nowadays we're all amateur psychologists and psychiatrists. We all presume to know the motives of men. But do we? In the last analysis, the only way you can judge by is results, and the man who uses his wealth for worthy causes, even ostentatiously, is better than the man who uses it only for ostentation. Yours is a very cynical view of the temple, if you don't mind my saying so, Mr. Gorfinkle. But cynicism is only disappointed idealism. We Jews speak of ourselves as a nation of priests, and it would follow that if we were completely true to our ideal, we would spend all our time in the temple in study and worship. We even tried it. In the small ghetto towns of Poland and Russia, there were those who did just that. But someone had to work, and it was usually the wives. I don't think I care for that. It's one of my objections to the monastery and the convent. I don't think the best way to live in the world is to avoid it. Ours is a practical religion, in which *parnossah,* making a living, is as important as prayer, and the world as important as the temple."

*If he says something that you can show is similar to your position, point it out to him, even if you have to twist his words a little to make it fit. The psychology of that is that he's anxious to get off the hook, and you're giving him a face-saving out.*

"Then why," Gorfinkle interposed swiftly, "have you consistently objected to our program, Rabbi? It's what we want, that the membership realize the temple is part of the world and has a role to play in the world."

"I don't object to your program as a program, although I think each individual should decide these things for himself. What concerns me is that it tends to antagonize the other party to the point

194

where there is danger that they will actually leave the temple organization. I have seen signs of it for some time at the board meetings. In all fairness, the other side has been equally intemperate. There has been little or no discussion on the merits of issues these last few months. Rather, what your side has proposed the others have opposed, and when they made suggestions, they were similarly treated by your group and for the same reason. No organization can survive that kind of feuding. In the last few days, however, you have discarded what little propriety you have up till now maintained. Mr. Brennerman's sermon —''

"What about his sermon?"

"He had no right to abuse the privilege of the pulpit in that way."

"Just a minute, Rabbi. I heard that speech, and you didn't. Taking it as a whole, I approved of it." Gorfinkle's lips turned up in his humorless smile.

"Then you are equally guilty, Mr. Gorfinkle."

"You forget that I am the president —''

"Of the temple organization, Mr.

Gorfinkle. The pulpit belongs to the rabbi."

"I didn't know that, Rabbi," said Gorfinkle mildly. "Is that Jewish law?"

"It is the law of common courtesy! As rabbi, I am superintendant of the religious school. Would I presume to take over a class from one of the teachers without first asking his permission?"

*It is sometimes worthwhile to yield a minor point.*

"Well, maybe Ted did get a little out of line. He's enthusiastic and gets carried away."

"And yesterday at the board meeting, you nominated Roger Epstein as chairman of the Ritual Committee."

"What's wrong with Roger Epstein?" Gorfinkle demanded indignantly.

"Nothing as a person. But he has had no temple background whatsoever and never attended one until coming here. The chairman of the Ritual Committee approves the order of the services. Under the circumstances, Mr. Paff's group, which tends toward Conservatism, might consider it a deliberate affront."

"Now hold on, Rabbi. I picked Roger because the Ritual Committee is the most important and he's my best friend. I'm not worried about his ignorance of the order of the service. I figure you and the cantor between you pretty much arrange that. But the chairman of the Ritual Committee distributes the honors on the holidays. Our people set great store by these honors and rightly so. I notice all the time Meyer Paff was chairman of the Ritual Committee he made political hay out of it. But while we're speaking of impropriety, Rabbi, how about the impropriety of getting a bunch of kids together, including my own son, and lecturing them on these matters from the opposition point of view? Isn't that abusing your privilege?"

"Kids? We accept the thirteen-year-old as a member of a minyan. He can be called to the reading of the Torah, which is instruction to the congregation. He can even lead the services. Can we say that bright young college people of eighteen and nineteen are too immature to understand what is going on in their temple community?"

"Look, Rabbi, I don't want any of your Talmudic run-around. I consider that politics, and I'm telling you I want it stopped."

The rabbi smiled. "You mean, you want me to stop talking to the young people?"

"I mean that you are not to talk to them about temple affairs. And I'm not asking you. I'm ordering you."

"You can't. *I* am the rabbi here, and it is for me to decide what I shall say to the members of the Jewish community."

*There comes a point in your discussion when you realize there's no chance of an agreement or reconciliation. When you reach that point, don't pussyfoot. Lower the boom and lower it all the way.*

Gorfinkle nodded. "You've said enough, Rabbi, to prove to me that you're part and parcel of Paff's apparatus. I'm not surprised. I suspected as much, as did the members of my group. We had a meeting last night, and I remind you that we represent a clear majority of the board. It was agreed that I was to talk to you and point out to you the impropriety of your behavior in the hope of bringing about a change. That's what this little conference is all about. But when I give them the gist of this conversation, along with your cavalier attitude toward religion in general, which has just recently come to my attention, I am sure they will vote to terminate you association with us.

"Of course, you can fight it, but you're a smart man, and I'm sure you realize that for a rabbi to fight for his job and lose is to jeopardize his chances of getting another. I can tell you now that you will lose and that after that meeting you won't be rabbi any longer." He rose to his feet in sign that the conference was over.

"I did not get my *smicha* from you," said the rabbi, also rising, "and you can't withdraw it. I am the rabbi of the Jewish community of Barnard's Crossing. The temple pays me, but I am not the creature of the temple, and I do not need a temple or synagogue to fulfill my function."

Outside there was the loud and persistent sound of an automobile horn.

Gorfinkle shrugged. "I'm sorry, Rabbi," he said smoothly. "That's Stu now, and I have to go."

# 23

Wilcox, his collar unbuttoned, his tie unknotted, the ends hanging loose, sat back in his armchair, his legs resting on a hassock, at peace with the world. He could tell from the way it started that this was going to be one of those all-the-time-in-the-world trips, where time slowed down to a deep, throbbing rhythm. He could hear the slow, steady movement of the gears inside his watch. And then, as if in accompaniment, he heard the pealing of the doorbell, a deep, insistent throbbing. He rose to his feet to answer. It was no simple motion, but a whole series of adventures in which each part of his body, each member, played some significant role, like a complicated army maneuver, or like a ballet in which his arms and legs, his hands, his fingers all had separate roles.

All had to move at their appointed time. And although it seemed that the act of opening the door and admitting his visitor and then going back to his easy chair was a matter of hours, he had no feeling of exhaustion from this tremendous effort. The figure in the chair before him grew larger and larger, like an inflating balloon. And then smaller and smaller and then once again larger. And yet this shifting of outline was not alarming in any way. Amusing, rather, especially when he realized it was only the man's normal respiration he was watching. Thinking about it quite objectively he came to the conclusion that the man must have run up the stairs, because he seemed to be breathing heavily; there were beads of perspiration on his forehead that he could see individually course down from the hairline until they fell into and filled and overflowed a furrow on the man's brow and then spilled over to the next furrow, and the next, until finally they were dissipated in the hairy jungle of the man's eyebrow. The man was saying something that he could understand perfectly, but it seemed too utterly ridiculous to merit his attention. Something about having to park his car around the corner. Silly man. Why should that be of interest? And his difficulty in finding the apartment bell. Something about asking a woman which bell it was. What significance was there whether a woman knew which apartment it was or not. The man had a grievance. He understood it. He could understand it not merely in his mind, but it registered as waves of resentment on his very skin. And it was unpleasant. And he wanted an end to it. He spoke from a great distance, explaining for the silly creature. And it seemed that the other understood, for he rose from his chair. Not a bright person certainly. Not with man's intelligence. No. Nor the intelligence of a dog even. Or even of a much lower animal. Not even the intelligence of a worm. Perhaps a microbe, because instead of going toward the door as he was told he was coming toward him. Ah, he understood at last. The other was taking his leave formally. Should he rise? Should he offer his hand? But the man was reaching forward and taking not his hand, but both ends of his tie. Was this the way to take one's leave? Was this a new ceremony? And then he felt the stricture on his neck and then pain and pressure and pressure and pain.

And nothing.

# 24

Mr. Carter looked around the table slowly, and his eye came to rest on the empty place on his right. His wife at the foot of the table and his children ranged on either side, the two young boys on his right and the two girls on his left, all sat straight, their hands folded and resting on the edge of the table, waiting for him to say Grace.

"And where is Moses?" he asked.

"He hasn't come home yet," said his wife. "He went into Boston to apply for a job, and he may have stopped for a bite. He said he might be late."

"And didn't you tell him that I want him here for the evening meal? Doesn't he know it himself? And if he were detained, couldn't he call and tell us? Have we no telephone in the house?"

"Oh, Pa," said his wife, "what's the sense of fussing at the boy all the time. He might not have been handy to a telephone. Or he might have called and the line was busy. The way the girls use the phone, it's a wonder anyone can ever get through."

"I don't hold with members of a family coming in at any and all hours. This is a family, and it's going to stay a family. That's morality. When everyone flies off to wherever, and anyone eats anytime they've a mind to and wherever they happen to be, the family starts breaking up. The meal is a sacrament, and everyone who is part of this family is going to take part in it."

"He might have got caught in the storm," his wife suggested, "and waited until it ended. Most likely he saw he was going to be late and grabbed a bite somewhere and then went directly to the bowling alley. Come to think of it, I believe Moose said something about their wanting him to come in a little earlier Mondays."

"Enough," said her husband. "I will not wait any longer. I will now say Grace.

If he comes in after, then he will not eat. I will not allow any member of my family to eat here who has not heard a decent benediction pronounced.''

He looked around the table and saw that all heads were bowed. Then his hands clenched convulsively, and his eyes squeezed shut. For a full minute he was silent, his mind reaching out, out. Then he put his head back, directing his voice to the ceiling. ''Dear Lord, we thank Thee for Thy mercy in giving us sustenance to strengthen our bodies so that we may do Thy work. We have observed Your commandments, and on our board there is no creature's flesh but only the fruits of Thy good earth. If we have sinned in Your eyes, it is because we are weak and lacking in understanding. Forgive us, O Lord, and deal kindly with us.'' Then he nodded and said, ''I thank Thee, Lord, I am your servant, and I will obey.''

He opened his eyes and looked around him. ''Now we may eat.''

The family ate in silence. No one wanted to hazard a remark that might set Mr. Carter off, and all were anxious to get away from the table as soon as possible. Mr. Carter himself sat in moody silence, his eyes focused on his plate. And when the meal was finished and the dishes cleared away, the young people eased out of the dining room quickly.

Mr. Carter continued to sit at his place at the dining room table while he was aware of the noises from the kitchen as his wife and the girls worked at washing the dishes. His wife came into the room.

"It's still raining pretty hard, Pa," she said. "I was wondering if Michael were to take the car and ride downtown and see if Moose is around —"

He looked at her, and she found it hard to meet his gaze. "I'll go out looking for him," he said.

"Oh, I'm just a worrying old woman. There's no need for anyone to go. He'll be along pretty soon —"

The phone rang, and Sharon hurried to answer it.

"That's Moose now," said Mrs. Carter.

But Sharon returned to report, "It was the bowling alley. They want to know where Moose is and why he isn't there."

But Mr. Carter had already got into his raincoat and was striding out of the house. He paused just long enough in the garage to select a length of dowel rod. He whipped it through the air once or twice and then took his place behind the wheel of his car and set the rod carefully on the seat beside him.

# 25

The rabbi wanted time to collect his thoughts before going home, to decide what he would tell Miriam or rather how he would tell her. It had started to rain almost as soon as he got into his car, and now as he drove aimlessly through the streets of the town it was coming down hard, striking against the windshield faster than the wipers could swish it away. Every now and then the skies suddenly grew daylight bright, with blinding flashes of lightning followed almost immediately by the crash of thunder. It was frightening and yet, because it suited his mood, exhilarating as well.

He wanted to talk the matter over with someone before seeing Miriam, but there was no one in the town with whom he felt he could talk freely and openly unless it was — he could not help smiling — Hugh Lanigan, the pleasant, red-faced Irish chief of police. They had an honest, long-standing relationship, maybe, he thought wryly, because neither had anything to gain from the other. It struck him in a situation of this sort, where everyone in the congregation was on one side or the other, how isolated the rabbi was. Of course, there was Jacob Wasserman, who, as a sort of elder statesman of the congregation, tended to be above factions. They had always liked each other, and he respected the older man's judgment and understanding. Impulsively he drove to his house.

Mrs. Wasserman was a motherly woman, who, when she saw who it was, urged him — even taking him by the arm — to come in, come in.

"It's all right, Rabbi, so the rugs will get a little wet," she said, as he scraped his shoes against the cocomat.

"Who is it?" her husband called from inside. "The rabbi? Come in, Rabbi, come in. It must be a serious matter to bring you out on such a night. But I'm happy you came. Lately I haven't seen so much of you. It's not so easy for me to get to the minyan these days. You know how it is. If the weather is not so good I stay in bed a little longer. Becker is here with me. He had supper here tonight. If it's private you want to talk, he can keep my wife company in the kitchen. I wouldn't be jealous. But if it's temple business, then maybe you'd like him to hear, too."

"Yes, I think it might be a good idea," said the rabbi.

The old man led him into the living room, and his wife followed them. "Look, Becker, I got another visitor," he called. Then to his wife, "So why don't you get the rabbi a cup of tea?"

"I have just seen Mr. Gorfinkle," said the rabbi and told them what had transpired. He expected the news to come, frankly, as something of a bombshell. Instead, the men were surprisingly unmoved.

"You mean he threatened not to renew your contract in the fall?" asked Becker, as if to make sure he had all the facts straight.

"No, that he would recommend it be terminated now."

"He can't do that; you've got a contract. Besides, that's something that the full board has to vote on."

"So they pay him the remaining money," said Wasserman with a shrug, "and if Gorfinkle has a majority, what difference does it make if it comes before the full board or not?"

The rabbi expected Becker to react belligerently. Instead, he looked at Wasserman and said, "Shall I tell him?"

Again the old man shrugged his shoulders. "What would be a better time?"

"In a way, Rabbi," began Becker, "it's funny you coming here tonight. You see, today Meyer Paff came to see me. It looks as if there's going to be a split in the temple. And Paff wanted me and Wasserman to join him."

"And did you agree?"

"For us it's easy, Rabbi. As past presidents, we are both permanent members of the board. And to join another temple is just a matter of paying an extra membership fee. It's like a donation. Even when I was president, I was a member of the synagogue in Lynn, and Jacob here is a member both in Lynn and Salem. But in the course of telling me what was on his mind, you came up for discussion. Paff asked me to approach you about coming over, on a long-term contract and at an increase in salary. That's what I was discussing with Jacob just before you came in."

The rabbi looked over at Wasserman, but the old man's face was impassive. "I didn't think I was so great a favorite of Mr. Paff's," he said to Becker.

"Look, Rabbi, I won't try to kid you. I'm sure that although Paff appreciates your work here, his main object in making the offer is that he expects it will pull members. But what do you care if you're bettering yourself?"

"And would I be bettering myself, Mr. Becker?"

"By three thousand dollars a year and a long-term contract. Even if this row with Gorfinkle hadn't occurred, you wouldn't be sure that your contract would be renewed. I guess that's bettering yourself. If you're not sure, ask Mrs. Small, who buys the groceries."

But the rabbi replied, "As things now stand, Mr. Becker, I am the rabbi of the Jews of Barnard's Crossing. I am the rabbi of the community and not merely the rabbi of a particular temple. And that is the way I think of my function. A rabbi is not part of the temple furniture."

"But the cantor —"

"The cantor is different. He needs a temple, or at least a congregation, in order to exercise his function. Can he sing to himself? But a rabbi does not. No doubt, if the community continues to grow, sooner or later a Reform temple will be established and a portion of our members will split away from us to join it. And no doubt, they will get a rabbi. But that break will be for ideological reasons and hence justified. Their rabbi will be the rabbi of the Reform Jews of Barnard's Crossing, while I remain the rabbi of its Conservative Jews."

"But congregations do split," Becker insisted.

"All too often, perhaps. When the split was not on ideological grounds, it was apt to be geographical. Jews would begin moving out of one area into another, and because it was considered a breach of the Sabbath to ride to services, another temple would be set up in order to have a place of worship within walking distance of the new area. That, too, would be reasonable.

"But the split that you plan is neither ideological nor geographical. You will have the same kind of Jews in the new temple as in the old, and the services will be virtually similar. In effect, you are setting up a competing temple, and you would like me to be its rabbi. No, thank you. Nor would I remain in my present job under those conditions. A temple is not a business enterprise in which competition is good for trade. But you will come to think of your temple in that way, and you will force the same kind of thinking on Gorfinkle and his group. Come join our temple — we have air conditioning, softer seats. Our cantor has a better voice, and our rabbi delivers shorter and snappier sermons. Hold your

Bar Mitzvah or your wedding in our vestry. We give trading stamps."

"Now look here, Rabbi —"

"Mr. Paff doesn't need me. A temple doesn't need a rabbi, and a rabbi doesn't need a temple. The rabbi's functions in the temple — leading prayers and delivering sermons — are the most minor part of his duties. The first any thirteen-year-old boy can perform, and the second, isn't it for most a kind of relief to break the monotony and tedium of the service? No, Mr. Becker, I have no intention of being the extra added attraction of a new temple."

"But if Gorfinkle succeeds in voting you out —"

The rabbi looked at Wasserman in mute question.

The old man spread his hands. "In this world, Rabbi, you've got to make first a living. Here Paff offers you a job, at more money yet. All right, maybe the conditions aren't perfect. Where are they perfect? But it's a living; it's *parnossah*."

The rabbi bit his lip in vexation. He had assumed that Wasserman at least would understand. "And is Barnard's Crossing the only place where I can make a living? No, Mr. Wasserman, if this split goes through, I will not accept a contract from either Mr. Paff's or Mr. Gorfinkle's group. I will leave Barnard's Crossing."

# 26

As Stuart Gorfinkle drove back to the cookout from Lynn, he felt a totally unreasonable resentment against his parents, especially his father. Why were there always strings attached when his father let him have the car? They were only going to his Aunt Edith's to eat; his uncle could have picked them up. He wondered uneasily if the kids had been able to find shelter somewhere when the rain really pelted down. And the lightning, had it been as bad at the beach as on the drive to Lynn?

The rain had let up and now was little more than a heavy mist. At Tarlow's Point he stopped his car and plunged down the path. When he came to the little grove of pine trees, he could see the beach and that no one was there. From the litter, the empty beer cans, the wet cellophane wrappers, he knew that they had left unexpectedly and in a hurry.

Then he saw the arrow on the log. Carefully he made his way to the house and up the back steps. He put his ear to the door and listened hard but heard nothing. He circled the house, went up to the front door, and again listened, then essayed a timid knock. He waited, listening, and this time he thought he heard something. He knocked harder and called, "It's me, Stu. You kids there?"

Instantly the door was thrown open, and his friends crowded around the doorway.

"Hey, you had me going there for a while."

"We thought you weren't coming back. We left an arrow with lipstick. Did you see it?"

"How'd you get in?" Stu asked. "Was the door open?"

"Nah, we climbed in through a window in back."

"Well, we better get going," said Stu. "The cruising car goes by here, and they check the unoccupied houses. They got a list.''

They piled into the car, and Stu turned on the ignition. From in back Adam Sussman called, ''Say, how about Moose?''

''What about him?'' asked Stu.

''He's in there. He passed out, and we had to put him to bed.''

''We'd better get him. We can't leave him in there like that.''

''There's no room for him, especially the shape he's in.''

''He wasn't invited to this party.''

''Yeah, but he got us in out of the storm.''

''I want to go home,'' wailed one of the girls. ''My folks will be awfully worried.''

''Get going, Stu,'' said Bill Jacobs. ''We can swing back afterward and pick him up.''

Stu and Bill Jacobs took Didi home last, and Alan Jenkins went along because his motorcycle was parked in the Epstein garage. The house was dark when they arrived, and on the kitchen table Didi found a note from her mother: "Gone to the movies — maybe somewhere for coffee afterward."

"You guys want some coffee?" she asked.

"Yeah, I could use something hot," said Jacobs.

"I should be starting back," said Jenkins, "but — okay, I'll have some too."

"But what about Moose?" asked Stu.

"He'll keep," said Jacobs. He laughed harshly. "He's good for hours."

"The way he poured that stuff down —" Stu shook his head. "Still, you wouldn't think beer would have that effect on him. At school I've seen guys who drink the stuff practically all night —"

"It wasn't the beer," Bill Jacobs explained, "although he had quite a few of those. As soon as we got into the house, he found himself a bottle of Scotch. He did the same trick with that — you know, tossing his head back and taking it down. He must've polished off half the bottle in a couple of swallows."

"Half a bottle?" said Stu, marveling.

"And he passed out? Complete? Blotto? What'd you do, leave him lying on the floor?"

"On the floor?" Jacobs was indignant. "Hell no, on one of the beds."

"Well, like they say, on the floor he can't roll off," said Stu defensively.

Jenkins laughed, and Jacobs said grimly, "The way we laid him on the bed he won't roll anywhere."

"There was one of these plastic sheets," Jenkins explained, "and we wrapped him up real good."

"Just like you swaddle a baby in a blanket," Jacobs added with satisfaction.

Didi came in with coffee. They sipped it in silence, each immersed in his own thoughts for the moment.

Then Stu said suddenly, "Hey, how are we going to get back in? We're not going to have to go through the window, I hope? You shut the door."

"No sweat," said Bill Jacobs. "I left it on the latch."

Jenkins set his cup down and rose lazily to his feet. "I better be starting. Got to get up real early tomorrow."

"Hey," said Bill. "With Stu driving, I'm not sure I can handle Moose alone if he should start acting up. Can't you give us a hand?"

Jenkins smiled and shook his head. "You're asking the wrong party. Far as I'm concerned, he can stay there until he turns to green mold. If I was you cats, I'd forget about him."

As the roar of Jenkins' motorcycle died away, Stu said, "What was he so up tight about?"

Didi answered, "Moose was dumping on him most of the evening. Frankly, I don't blame Alan."

"Well, that leaves us in a bind," said Jacobs. He went to the window and looked out. "And it's started raining again."

They sat around and talked, waiting for the rain to let up. Every once in a while one of them would wander to the window to peer at the rain-lashed streets.

Suddenly a bolt of lightning flashed across the sky, followed immediately by a tremendous crash of thunder, and the room was plunged into darkness.

"That must have got a transformer," said Jacobs, looking down the darkened street. "Maybe the substation; it's dark all up and down the street."

"You got any candles, Didi?" asked Stu.

"I — I guess so." Didi's voice sounded frightened in the darkness, and then he felt her hand groping for his. He put his arm around her.

"Tell you what. Rather than sweat this out in darkness, why don't we all get in the car and drive over to pick up Moose now? The way it's coming down, it can't last long."

# 27

Mr. Morehead was apologetic. "Believe me, Mr. Paff, if I didn't have to meet my wife at the airport —"

"But I've arranged with the other men in the deal to meet them at the house. You could have let me know earlier."

"I didn't expect her until tomorrow, Mr. Paff. I just got a call from New York, from the airport. Look, you don't need me there anyway. You can get the key from —"

"Don't tell me to go to see that son of a bitch Begg again. He'll tell me he can't get away from his two-bit store and that he can't let me have the key because I might steal the furniture. Furniture! I've seen better at the Morgan Memorial. I'll drive up with a truck and load it with his goddam ratty furniture."

The other chuckled. "Begg is an old Yankee, all right. But look, how would it be if I left the key in Lynn?"

"Happens I've got to check something at the Lynn alley."

"Well, that's fine then. You know the drugstore on the corner where my building is? I'll leave the key there, and you can pick it up."

"Well, I guess that's all right. You just be sure that there's no slipup. Give them my name and tell them what I look like so there won't be any question when I come in for it."

"Nothing to worry about, Mr. Paff. And you look over the property as long as you like. Just be sure you turn out the lights and lock the door when you leave."

At the Lynn alley the manager greeted him with, "Your wife just called, Mr. Paff, and said for you to call a Mr. Kermit Arons."

Arons was remorseful. "Gee, Meyer, you'll never guess what I went and did. After I made this appointment with you for tonight I forgot all about my sister-in-law's wedding anniversary. She's throwing a big shindig, and if I don't go to it, well, I might just as well start discussing visitation rights to the children with my lawyer. So for tonight, I'm afraid you'll have to count me out."

"But we've got to act fast on this thing, Kerm. We can't futz around."

"So act. What do I know about buildings, anyway? If you guys say it's all right, then it's all right with me. I'll go along with whatever you decide."

As soon as he hung up, the manager bore down on him. "Look, Mr. Paff, Moose is late again. I called his house, and he wasn't home. I haven't eaten yet."

"Well, why don't you go out and grab a bite. I'll cover for you, and I'll get somebody for tonight. Frank over at the Malden Alley said he could work any night except Friday."

"Well, what if Moose comes in?"

"If he comes in while I'm here, I'll fire him. And if he doesn't show up, I'll tell him tomorrow he's through. Look, don't take too long; I've got an appointment."

"Sure, Mr. Paff, I'll just get a

hamburger and a cup of coffee. Say, I know a young fellow who if you hire him, I know he'd be reliable and —"

"We'll talk about it. You go and eat now."

He started for the door, but Paff called after him, "Say, have the cops been in again since —"

"Oh, don't worry about them, Mr. Paff. I know how to handle *them.*"

"Well, that's what I wanted to tell you. Lay off. Don't rile them. Understand?"

"Oh, sure, Mr. Paff."

"Don't act flip. Just cooperate."

While the other was gone, the phone rang. It was Dr. Edelstein. "Meyer? Your wife gave me this number, and said I might catch you here. I just got a call, and I got to go clear down to Lawrence for a consultation."

"But, Doc, Kermit Arons can't make it. He got to go to his sister-in-law's anniversary party, and now you —"

"It's a man's life, Meyer."

Parked under the streetlamp opposite Hillson House, Meyer Paff decided that he would wait just five more minutes for Irving Kallen and then leave. It was easier to get money out of his friends than work, he reflected bitterly. He was not merely annoyed; he was physically uncomfortable. Because of the rain he had to keep the car window up, and it was hot and sticky inside. He could have gone into the house — he had the key — but he remembered what Begg had said about vandals having broken in there on occasion, and he did not want to go in alone. Besides, half-hidden behind its overgrown hedge, the house now looked dark and forbidding. And the thunder and lightning didn't help things any.

He glanced at his watch and saw that he had been there almost half an hour. He looked uncertainly down the road and, seeing no car approaching, turned on the ignition and drove off.

# 28

". . . No ma'am, you notify the electric company. But I can tell you there's no need to call them either. They know about it. The power is out in all that part of town. The storm knocked out the substation."

Sergeant Hanks turned to Patrolman Smith, who had unbuttoned his tunic and was relaxing with a cup of coffee. "Boy, what a night! Must be a hundred people calling the electric company and then calling us when they can't get *them*."

Smith smiled sympathetically, but the sergeant was back at the phone again. "Barnard's Crossing Police Department, Sergeant Hanks speaking . . . Yes, Mr. Begg . . . Oh yes, that's one of the houses the cruising car checks regular . . . No sir, nothing was called in . . . You say it was lit up? . . . That's funny — all power in that part of town is out. You don't have lights, do you? . . . Oh, before . . . No, sir, I was not talking to my girl and not to my wife either . . . Well, I'm sorry about that, but people been calling in almost constantly for the last hour or so about the lights . . . Yes sir, I'll have the cruising car check. . . ."

He wheeled around in his swivel chair. "Son of a bitch!"

"Begg? No two opinions on him," said the patrolman. "Did I ever tell you about the time he —"

"I better call the cruising car," the sergeant interrupted. "It would be just like him to keep tabs on the time. Hear me, Bob? . . . Hanks . . . When did you pass Tarlow's Point? . . . Uh-huh . . . Well, take a run down there, will you? Old man Begg claims he saw a light there . . . No, just before the transformer blew . . . Okay."

# 29

They drove three in the front seat, Didi between the two boys. Stu turned the wipers to high speed to take care of the rain lashing against the windshield. "I sure don't envy that Jenkins riding a motorcycle in this kind of weather."

"Oh, he can always duck in someplace until it lets up," said Jacobs.

They parked in front of Hillson House, and Stu dug a flashlight out of the glove compartment and snapped on the beam.

"Hey," said Jacobs, "the door is open."

"Maybe Moose woke up and just walked out," said Stu hopefully.

"Could be, but we better take a look around. Here, let me have the flash." Bill mounted the stairs with Stu behind him. He pushed open the front door and cast the light around the room. Then he led the way down the hall to the study, where they had left Moose. He stopped at the threshold and focused the beam on the couch. What looked like a giant cocoon in silvery white plastic was resting on top of it.

Stu giggled nervously. "Geez, you sure wrapped him good. What did you put it over his head for?"

But Jacobs was already at the couch. "We didn't leave him like that. Help me!"

The figure was completely encased in the sheet, the top flap of which had been folded over the head and tucked tightly into the folds enwrapping the body.

Jacobs yanked at the flap frantically and then, with Stu's help, pulled the rest of the sheet from the body. The face was curiously white. Jacobs felt the forehead and cheeks. They were cold. He handed the flashlight to Stu and began to rub the hands of the figure on the couch. Then he dropped them in distaste.

"What's the matter?" Stu whispered.

"I think he's dead."

He thrust his hand underneath the shirt to see if he could feel a heartbeat.

"You can't tell that way," said Stu. "You got to hold something like a mirror up to his lips."

"I haven't got a mirror," said Bill savagely. "Put the lens of the flash to his mouth."

Stu offered the flashlight, but Bill said, "Let's get the hell out of here."

They started to walk out and then broke into a run. They clattered down the steps and then raced to the car. Stu pulled the car door open while Bill ran around the front to the other side.

"Where's Moose?" asked Didi as she moved over to let Stu get behind the wheel.

"Never mind." He turned on the ignition, but before he could shift to DRIVE a car zoomed toward them, veered over, and came to a stop immediately in front, its headlights on high beam shining in their eyes. Stu's door was pulled open by a policeman with a gun in his hand. "Hold it," he commanded. "Now come out, all of you."

# 30

Harvey Kanter, Ben Gorfinkle's brother-in-law, was ten years his senior. Although in private he was radical, atheistic, and irreverent, in public, as the managing editor of the Lynn *Times-Herald,* he was Republican, conservative, and a staunch defender of the status quo. He wrote editorials supporting book censorship, prayers in the schools, law and order in the cities, and attacked student rioting, the coddling of criminals, and the hippie movement. He was a tall, rangy man, with a shock of iron-gray hair brushed back impatiently. Everything about him was impatient. He was nervous, fidgety; he could not sit still; he either got up and paced the floor, or if he remained seated, he would slide forward to rest on the end of his spine or pull a leg under him or slouch around if the chair permitted it so that his head was on one arm and his legs on the other.

His attitude toward Gorfinkle tended to be mocking and derisive, and his wife, Edith, was also apt to be somewhat patronizing to her younger sister, Mrs. Gorfinkle. Nevertheless, the Gorfinkles came to dinner when they were invited, partly as a matter of habit and partly because in a perverse kind of way Ben Gorfinkle enjoyed the discussions.

After dinner the two men lounged into the living room while the women cleared the table and proceeded to wash the dishes. Kanter bit off the end of a cigar, and as he held a match to the end he said, "I heard your rabbi the other day. Did I tell you?"

"No," said Gorfinkle cautiously. "When was that?"

"About a week ago. He was the speaker at the Chamber of Commerce meeting, save the mark."

"I didn't think you went to those."

"Hell, the paper has to be represented, and I drew the short straw. Your man wasn't bad."

"What did he talk about?"

"Oh, the usual — the place of the temple in the modern world. Seems to me I've heard a dozen priests and ministers and such godly folk at one affair or another in the last six months, and all they talk about is the place of the church, or in this case the synagogue, in the modern world. I figure if they talk about it so much, it's because it ain't so, but your guy seemed to make some sense."

"What did he say?"

"Oh, the point of his talk, as I remember it, was that the modern civilized world was finally coming around to the positions that the synagogue had been preaching for a couple of thousand years or more — social justice, civil rights, rights of women, importance of learning. His idea was that finally, after nearly two thousand years, the Jewish religion was coming into style."

"That's very interesting," said Gorfinkle. "I had a long talk with him — just before I came here, as a matter of fact. And it was about somewhat the same subject, but he took what I thought was the opposite point of view in his discussion with me. I guess there are some people who can take either side of a discussion, depending on how it suits them," he added.

"He didn't strike me as that type of man," said Kanter quietly. "What happened?"

"Well, you know, as in any organization, we have two parties — mine and what you might call the opposition, which is headed by Meyer Paff. You know him."

"Yeah, I know him."

"Well, we want the temple to get active in various movements that are current — like civil rights, for one. Paff's bunch want to keep it a place where — you know — you just come to pray on the High Holidays or on Friday nights. And I found out that the rabbi was carrying on some pretty active propaganda for the Paff group. So I had it out with him."

"And how did it end?"

"I told him in no uncertain terms that I wasn't going to stand for it and that the group that I represented — and we're a clear majority — weren't going to stand for it.'' He leaned forward in his chair. "You see, what he was doing was talking to the kids — telling them that we were in the wrong. He's kind of popular with the kids, and he was planning to use them to influence their parents.''

"How did he take it?''

"Oh, he got on his high horse and said no one was going to tell him what to say, that he was the rabbi and he would decide what was proper for him to say and what wasn't.''

"So?''

Gorfinkle was pleasantly conscious that he had captured his brother-in-law's interest and that, for once, what he was about to say would startle him out of his customary superciliousness. He smiled. "So I told him that I'd had a meeting with a majority of the board prior to our little talk and that we had decided that if he refused to go along, at the next meeting a motion would be offered — and passed — calling for his resignation.''

"You fired him?''

He pursed his lips and canted his head

to one side. "Just about."

"Nothing personal, of course."

"I flatter myself that I handled it pretty well," said Gorfinkle with a smirk.

Kanter got up from his chair and strode across the room. He turned and glared down his long nose at his brother-in-law. "By God, you nice respectable people can blunder into a situation and foul it up to make the angels weep. You get elected president, and before you have a chance to warm your arse on the chair you start firing people."

"An organization can't go in two directions at the same time," Gorfinkle protested. "If we're going to make any progress —"

"Progress? Why in hell do you have to make progress? Do you think everything has a balance sheet that has to be matched against the balance of the previous year to show you're going ahead? What the hell kind of progress does an institution that has lasted a couple of thousand years have to make?"

"If it's to be a living institution —"

"It's got to hop aboard the bandwagon,

is that it? Civil rights, slum clearance, job opportunities — they're all in style now and respectable, so all the bleeding-heart liberals and social democrats try to get in on the act. Faugh! You guys make me sick. When did you get to be so goddam liberal? How many blacks have you hired at Hexatronics?''

"I don't do the hiring."

"But of course you picket the office of the one who does."

"I don't notice any great liberalism in the policy of the *Times-Herald,*" said Gorfinkle drily, "and *you* run that."

"I run it for the owners. And I run it their way. Oh, I'm a prostitute, all right," he added cheerfully. "Most newspaper men have to be. But I don't fool myself. A prostitute yes, but no hypocrite."

"Well, I have reason to believe that Rabbi Small is, which had something to do with my decision," said Gorfinkle smugly.

"Doesn't wrap his phylacteries properly? Wears his prayer shawl inside out?"

"I had no idea you were so concerned

about rabbis and things religious," said Gorfinkle.

"I'm not, and I hardly know your rabbi. I just don't like to see people hurt." He studied his brother-in-law for a moment. "And the effect on the congregation? Have you thought about that?"

Gorfinkle shrugged. "He really has no following, except maybe among the kids, and they don't count. As a matter of fact, it was the congregation I was thinking of when I had this talk with him. Fact is," he lowered his voice, "I was trying to prevent a serious split in the congregation. You see, there is this handful of dissidents — the old guard — who are opposed to every aspect of our program. Well, they'll either knuckle under or they'll get out. If they leave, it doesn't bother us too much; they're just a couple or three dozen of them. But if we let the rabbi continue, he might stir up enough opposition so that we could lose a hundred or more. That would be serious."

"So the strategy is to silence the opposition?"

"What's wrong with that? Why should we furnish the opposition with a rostrum?"

"Because it's democratic. The government does it."

They argued long and frequently loudly; and when, quite late, the Gorfinkles finally prepared to depart, neither man had convinced the other. They said their good-byes with formal politeness no different from the way any number of their discussions had ended in the past.

Five minutes after they had left, the phone rang and Harvey Kanter answered.

"Barnard's Crossing Police Department, Sergeant Hank speaking. May I speak to Mr. Benjamin Gorfinkle?"

"He's just left."

"Is he on his way home, sir?"

"Sure, I guess so. What's this all about?"

"We'll get in touch with him there."

"Just a minute. I'm his brother-in-law, Harvey Kanter of the *Times-Herald*. Was there an accident? Was his place broken into?"

"No, Mr. Kanter, nothing like that."

And the sergeant hung up, leaving Kanter wondering uneasily what he should do.

# 31

Sergeant Herder of the Boston Police Department was a man of infinite patience, and he found himself forced to use every bit of it as he dealt with the slattern before him. "Now, look, Madelaine, let's see if we can get a little cooperation. Remember what I told you: That man knows you saw him leave the Wilcox place, and he might get worried about it and try to do something drastic. Do you understand?"

The woman, her eyes fixed on him as though hypnotized, nodded her head rapidly.

"What do you understand?"

"He might try to do something."

"What?"

She shook her head. "I don't know."

Sergeant Herder got up and walked

rapidly to the end of the room. He stood there for a moment, gazing at the wall. Then he came back slowly. "He might try to kill you, Madelaine, the way he did Wilcox. That's what he might try to do."

"Yes, sir."

"Yes, sir, what?"

"He might try to kill me."

"Fine. Just remember that. Just keep that in mind. So we've got to get him before he has the chance. And to get him, we have to know what he looks like. See?"

"I know what he looks like."

"I know you do, but we don't unless you tell us. Now what size man was he? Was he a big man or small?"

"Sort of middling."

"What color hair did he have?"

"He had his hat on."

"All right, what color hat was it?"

"Just a man's hat."

"Just a hat. Fine. Now Officer Donovan here is an artist, Madelaine. He draws pictures."

"I know what an artist is," she said with dignity.

"Sure you do. Now we're getting somewhere. Officer Donovan is going to show you some outlines of faces, and I want you to tell him which one looks most like the man's, the man we're talking about, the man you saw. Understand?"

She nodded.

"Show her one with a hat, Donovan."

She looked at the outline. "The hat was squashier," she said.

"How about the outline of the face?"

"Yeah, that could be it."

"Fine. Now we're getting somewhere."

"Just a minute," said Donovan. He sketched rapidly and presented another outline to her, quite different from the first. "How about this one?"

"Yeah, that could be it."

"Maybe you ought to try her on the mug shots again," suggested Donovan.

Herder shook his head in total frustration.

"I'm sure she'd know him if she saw him. She just can't describe him."

"By now, I'm not sure she even saw him."

"It was the same way with the other

one, the football player, but she picked his picture out of the bunch we handed her."

"Yeah." He turned back to the woman. "Now, Madelaine, I'm going to show you a bunch of pictures and you tell me if you see him. All right?"

"Sure, Sergeant, anything you say."

# 32

When the telephone rang, Mrs. Carter was sure it was Moose. But there was a strange voice at the other end.

"Mr. Carter, please," it said.

"Mr. Carter isn't in just now," she replied. "Can I take a message?"

"This is the Barnard's Crossing Police Department calling. Can you tell me where we can reach Mr. Carter? When do you expect him?"

"He went out right after supper," she said. "Just a minute, I hear a car driving in. Maybe that's him now. Hold the line a minute."

She heard the door open and she called out, "Is that you, Raphael? You're wanted on the telephone."

He picked up the receiver. "Carter speaking," he said.

"This is the Barnard's Crossing Police Department. Lieutenant Jennings. Will you please wait for our Sergeant Hanks. He'll be right over."

"Police Department? What's this all about?"

"Sergeant Hanks will explain," said the voice at the other end, followed by a click as Lieutenant Jennings hung up.

# 33

"Damn funny, all your folks should be out for the evening," said Chief Lanigan. "What time are they expected back?"

Stu shrugged.

Didi said, "All I know is I found a note on the kitchen table saying they were going to a movie. They didn't say which one, but I know it wasn't the Seaside in Barnard's Crossing because they already saw that one. And then they might go on someplace for coffee."

"Well, I'll just have the sergeant keep calling every fifteen minutes or so until we get them. You kids wait right here and don't try anything funny."

And he left them sitting in his office, the two boys on a bench by the wall, Didi in an armchair near the window. She looked forlorn and puffy-eyed. The shock of hearing of the death of a boy she had seen only a few hours before, followed by her arrest, had unnerved her completely. She had control of her emotions now, however, and stared moodily out the window at the little grass plot in front of the station house.

Stu edged closer to Bill Jacobs and whispered, "You know, I don't think they're going to let us go without our folks coming down. Maybe I ought to tell them that they're at my Aunt Edith's, and that he can reach them there."

"You already told them you didn't know," Bill whispered back.

"No, I didn't. He asked us if we knew what time they are coming back, but he didn't ask us where they were."

"I think we should sit tight. Maybe when he calls and finds our folks are out, he'll let us go."

Stu sat back, unhappy, his fingers drumming nervously on the arm of the bench. He edged forward again. "You know what, Bill? I think we ought to tell them about Moose — I mean, about how we found him."

"Sure, why not? *You're* in the clear," said Bill bitterly. "It doesn't matter to you."

"What does that mean?"

"Well, you weren't in the house at all during the storm. And he was dead already when you showed up. But where does that leave me and Didi?"

"But they're going to find out sooner or later."

"How are they going to find out? From what I overheard the cops talking, they think he just died from an overdose of alcohol."

"Yeah, but that's just the cops. Once a doctor examines the body, he'll know he didn't die that way. He'll be able to tell whether a guy died of alcohol or from suffocation."

"I don't mean we shouldn't tell them," Bill temporized, "but I don't think we have to tell them anything without a lawyer. And they can't count it against us," he said with an assurance he did not feel. "That's the law."

"Maybe you're right. I wish my old man were here," said Stu unhappily.

"He'd raise hell with me for getting involved, but he'd know what to do. He'd see that the cops treated us fair. Say, who do you think could have done it?"

Bill shook his head. "I left the door unlatched. Anybody could have come in."

"Hey, how about this Alan Jenkins? You all said Moose was leaning on him from the minute he laid eyes on him. These days they don't take that lying down."

"And he left Didi's house in plenty of time to swing back there."

"I know."

# 34

"What did you expect him to say, David? Mr. Wasserman is an old man; he's practical. I know how you feel, but sometimes you have to compromise. You yourself have said that *parnossah* is necessary for a good life, that you can't have a good life unless you're making a living." She had fussed over him like a mother hen, bringing him his slippers and pouring him a cup of hot tea liberally laced with whisky and lemon. "Drink it; it will ward off a cold."

"Making a living is a necessity," he said through her ministrations. "Making a good living is a luxury. I don't need luxury for a good life. I don't reject it, of course; I am not ascetic. But I don't need it."

"But wherever you go, except in small

towns like Barnard's Crossing, there will be more than one temple. And that will mean competition."

He shook his head wearily. "You don't understand, Miriam. In the nature of things the rabbi is paid by a temple or synagogue because here in America it's the most practical way of compensating him for his work. But he is not the employee of the temple, just as a judge is compensated by the state but is still completely free to rule against it in an action. And if his courthouse burns down, it doesn't mean that he loses all function and responsibility and purpose. But here, if the temple should split, we would have an ugly situation. The rabbis of the two institutions would become bargaining points in the two campaigns for membership. And I want no part of it."

"But if, as you say, you insist on being the rabbi for the entire community, it means living in a small town."

"Well, I like small towns. Don't you?"

"Ye-es, but small towns mean small communities, and small communities mean small pay. Don't you have any personal ambition?''

He looked at her in surprise. ''Of course. Why else would I spend so much time at my studies? But my ambition is to be a rabbi, not something else. I have no interest in using the rabbinate as a springboard to some other kind of work that pays more and carries greater prestige. I don't think I'd care to be a big rabbi with a big pulpit at some prestigious temple where I could never be found because I'd have speaking engagements all the time. I wouldn't like it, and'' — he reached over and patted her hand reassuringly — ''you wouldn't like it either. Maybe you'd be proud of me for a little while, seeing my name or my picture in the Jewish press. But after a while you'd get used to that, like everything else. Besides, I don't think I could do it, anyway.''

''But you have to do some compromising, David, or —''

''Or what?''

''Or keep moving.''

''We've been here almost six years. But you're right, we can't keep moving. It's not good for Jonathan, for one thing. And I've been thinking about it. Wherever I go, there will be other Gorfinkles and other Paffs."

"So what do you plan to do?" she asked quietly.

He shrugged. "Oh, one day this week I'll go down to New York and see Hanslick and tell him that I would like another position. I might look into the possibility of Hillel work —"

"David, is that why you are being so" — she was going to say stubborn, but decided on another word — "so resolute about this situation here?"

He gave her a sharp look and then smiled. "Catholics have their confessors," he said, "and Jews have their wives. I think I like our arrangement better."

"You're dodging me," she said but laughed in spite of herself.

"Am I? Yes, I suppose I am. Well, I think perhaps that is part of the reason. Didn't you like it — the two days in Binkerton? To tell the truth, dear, I'm tired of fighting. I've been doing it for almost six years, ever since I came here. I was prepared for a certain amount of it, but I thought that once it was established just who was the rabbi here, I'd be able to concentrate on my real job. But throughout my tenure, I've had to fight just to stay. I tell you I'm tired of it."

"You had an argument at Binkerton," she observed.

"That was different. That was a matter of principle. I don't know, maybe this is the wrong congregation for me. They're so — so contentious." He thrust his hands deep into his trouser pockets and strode the floor.

"Well, Jews have never been known as a passive people," Miriam said gently. "And what makes you think their sons and daughters in the colleges will be any different?"

"Perhaps not, but I'm hoping their disagreements would be over issues of greater moment than whether or not to have permanent seating arrangements, say. But it's more than that. A rabbi is primarily a student, a scholar. And for scholarship, a certain amount of leisure is necessary. In Hillel work, I'm hoping I would have the time —"

"But here you're doing things; in the college you'd only be reading about them."

"Well, I'd like a chance to do a little reading."

"Oh, you —" She controlled herself. "Your head is in the clouds, David. What about the immediate future? The community seder on Sunday, for instance. Will you be running it? Have you thought of that?"

"No, I haven't. But now that you mention it, I suppose that until I resign or am voted out I'm still the rabbi officially, and I would preside. Of course, Gorfinkle through his new Ritual Committee could decide to have the cantor run it, or Brooks, for that matter. It wouldn't bother me too much. As a lame-duck rabbi, I might find it embarrassing. Besides, the seder is not really a community affair. It's a family affair. The only reason we have a seder in the temple is because a lot of our members are either too lazy to run their own or feel that they can't."

"But if they did arrange for someone else to run it, what would you do?"

"Do? I'd stay home."

"But —"

The doorbell rang.

"Who can that be at this hour?" exclaimed the rabbi. "It's eleven o'clock."

Miriam hurried to the door. "Why, it's Mr. Carter. Come in, won't you."

He permitted himself to be led into the room and sat down on the chair that was drawn up for him. He sat on the edge, his back straight and not touching the chairback. "My son is dead," he announced.

A shocked glance passed between the rabbi and his wife.

"Oh, Mr. Carter, I'm so sorry," said Miriam.

"How did it happen?" asked the rabbi quietly. "Tell me about it. Is there anything I can do?"

"Maybe there is," said Carter. "They called me tonight. I was out, and they called just as I was coming in the house. Asked me to wait until some police sergeant got there. When he came, he wanted me to go down the station with him. I kept asking him what is the matter, and all he would say was that I'd find out when I got to the station house. The chief was there when I got there, and he told me. He wanted me to identify the body." He gave a short bitter laugh. "My boy's picture was in the paper practically every week last year. I'll bet that most people in town knew him better than the chairman of the Board of Selectmen. He was the guest of honor at the annual banquet of the Junior Chamber of Commerce at the end of the football season. But they needed me to identify him."

"That's just necessary formality, I believe," remarked the rabbi.

"Yuh, I guess so."

"Did they tell you how he had met his death?"

"They didn't say positive except that he had been drinking, that it looked like he had been drinking an awful lot. Well, that stuff is poison. He was intoxicated, that's what he was. That's a Latin word, and it means poison. Did you know that?"

The rabbi nodded.

"They took the body down to the police station," Carter went on, "in the police ambulance. They opened the door and there he was, with a blanket over him. The head was toward the front of the car, so I had to climb right in. Lanigan got in after me, and he pulled back the blanket. 'Is that your son?' he asks. And I says, 'Yes, that's my son.' So then they told me how they found him at Hillson House. He was lying on a couch there, and they could smell the whisky on him. Lanigan said how if you drink the stuff fast enough before the body has a chance to get rid of it, it can be very dangerous. So I guess that's what must have happened."

"You said you thought I could help," said the rabbi. "Did you want me to try to get further information on just how it happened?"

The carpenter shook his head, "No, I guess that's how it happened, the way Lanigan said. I knew that Moose drank even when he was in high school." He paused again and then went on. "Lanigan drove me home and left me to break the news to Mrs. Carter. She carried on

264

something dreadful. Lanigan called a doctor, and he gave her something to quiet her. I didn't have the heart to prevent it, God forgive me."

"And how is she now?" asked Miriam gently.

"Well, right now she's asleep. My oldest girl is with her." He knuckled his eyes, as if to wipe the sleep out of them. "Then I went back to the station house — Lanigan had left earlier — to make arrangements to get the body so I could give it decent burial. And Lanigan told me that they might have to do an autopsy on him to find out for sure what the cause of death was."

"I suppose that's the law," said the rabbi.

"Well, I don't hold with it. I know the cause of death. Lanigan told me. So why do they have to cut him open?"

"I suppose they have to be sure."

"How much surer do they have to be than they are right now? The body is the temple of the spirit, Rabbi. Even if the spirit is gone, do you have a right to destroy the temple? I don't hold with it.

265

It's against my religious beliefs." He fixed piercing eyes on the rabbi. "Now, I'm not looking for a fight with the police department or with the town, but if I have to fight, I will. But I've heard that you're friendly with Lanigan and have been almost since you came. I thought maybe you could speak to him about it for me."

"I have no legal standing in the matter," said the rabbi. "I mean, I'm not a lawyer, and I couldn't act as your legal representative. Have you thought of getting a lawyer?"

Carter shook his head. "It's not a fight I want right now, Rabbi. When it comes to going to court, I'll get a lawyer. Right now I'm thinking whether you could persuade him for my sake and my wife's sake."

"All right, I'll talk to him," said the rabbi. "But I wouldn't expect too much. Lanigan isn't the sort of man who would refuse a request of this kind unless he had a very good reason and saw it as a necessary duty. And if that is so, then I don't think I could persuade him. But I'll talk to him if you like."

"When?" asked Carter pointedly.

"Anytime you like."

"How about now? Tonight?"

# 35

"Did you make contact with the Hillsons?" asked Lanigan.

Lieutenant Jennings nodded. "Sort of contact," he amended. "I spoke to the housekeeper. A regular battle-ax. She said the girls — girls, the younger one is seventy-five! — anyway, they were asleep and she wasn't going to wake them, and I ought to be ashamed to be calling this time of the night, and she didn't care if I were the police or the United States Army."

"She said that? The United States Army?"

"Her words, Hugh. She even banged the receiver down once, but I called back" — he nodded in self-satisfaction — "and I told her that she better stay on the line until I got through with her, or I'd notify the local police to go out there and pick her up and bring her here. She must have believed me, because she didn't try it again. Then she wanted to know what had happened, and when I told her that I didn't have time to give her all the details, she said she was going to call the police, her police. Anyway, she finally told me that the house was up for sale and was in the hands of the Bellmore Realty Company of Lynn, who were the sole agents. Fortunately, I remembered that Bellmore was originally Bell and Morehead and that John Morehead lives here in town. So I called him and he told me that he was supposed to meet a group who were interested in buying the property at the house at half past eight, that he had given the key to one of them because something had come up and he wouldn't be able to meet them."

"Did he say who they were?"

"He didn't know, except the man he gave the key to. He was the only one he'd be dealing with, anyway."

"And who was that?"

"Meyer Paff. He's the —"

"Yeah, I know, the bowling alley man."

"Sure. He's got one in Lynn and Revere, all over the map, as far up as Gloucester."

Lanigan's eyes were shining. "And just the other day Kevin O'Connor called me to ask what I knew about him. The Lynn police have been watching that alley of his for pot."

"Hell, they watch every place where kids hang around, and kids hang around bowling alleys."

"Yes, but look here. We find pot on Moose, and he's dead. And we find there's a witness that can swear that earlier in the day he visited this guy Wilcox in Boston. And Wilcox was suspected of dealing in pot. And he's dead. And where do we find Moose? In Hillson House. And now here's Meyer Paff, who owns a place that the Lynn police suspect is a distribution point for pot. And Moose Carter works for Paff. And Meyer Paff has a key to Hillson House. And what's more, he had an appointment to meet some people there tonight."

"Yeah, but most of that is just coincidence."

"Sure, and it was just the coincidence of both having some connection with pot that led me to call the Boston police, which is how we found out that Moose had been to see this Wilcox earlier in the day. Have you called Paff yet?"

Through his pale-blue, watery eyes Lieutenant Jennings looked reproachfully at his chief. "I just finished talking to John Morehead, Hugh."

"All right. That's fine. Go dig him up."

"You mean tonight? Right now?"

"Sure. Bring him down and let him make a statement. He'll sleep better for it."

Jennings grinned. "Gotcha."

# 36

Chief Lanigan was startled when he saw his visitor. "You psychic or something, Rabbi?"

"What do you mean?"

Lanigan's broad red face relaxed in an easy smile. He ran a hand through his short white hair and eased back in his swivel chair. Although the smile remained on his face, his candid blue eyes were guarded. "Always happy to see you, you know that, but I'm sure you wouldn't come down to the station on a rainy Monday night just to say hello. Or were you passing by?"

"I'm here about Moose Carter. His father —"

"Don't tell me Carter is a member of your congregation," said Lanigan with a grin. "You know, you have no standing in the matter, Rabbi."

"I'm here at his request. Surely that gives me some position."

"Some, but not enough." His grin broadened.

The rabbi could not understand Lanigan's attitude, but he plunged ahead. "You told Carter that his son had died of alcohol poisoning. All right, he accepts your finding, and now all he wants is to give him a proper burial. As I understand it, you refuse to surrender the body, and you hinted to him that you might order an autopsy. He has strong principles on the matter. His religious convictions are opposed to the idea."

"Religious convictions? Hell, the guy's a nut."

"He's not as crazy as you think. He would not oppose an autopsy if it meant finding out the cause of death, but here you know the cause of the death."

"And that's where you're wrong, Rabbi. I told him I thought it was alcohol poisoning, but I didn't say we were certain. There's an awful lot that needs explaining. Did you know the boy?"

The rabbi shook his head.

"He was a big boy, over two hundred pounds, and alcohol poisoning, you know, depends a good deal on body size. It takes more of the stuff to have the same effect on a big man than it would on a little man. The way it works — if you take enough of it and you take it fast enough before the body can get rid of it — the nerve controlling the breathing apparatus is paralyzed, and you're asphyxiated. And on the basis of the available evidence, it just doesn't look as if he had enough to kill him. And there are other angles. Come with me, and I'll show you something."

He led the way into a small room off the front entrance. From a filing cabinet he drew a large manila envelope and emptied its contents on a table. He held up a plastic tobacco pouch, unrolled it, and passed it to the rabbi. "What do you think of that?"

The rabbi sniffed at it and then took a pinch of the greenish flakes. Gingerly he touched it with the tip of his tongue.

"Careful, Rabbi, you're breaking the law."

"Then this is —"

"Grass, pot, Mary Jane, marihuana. We found that in Moose's trouser pocket. And here's his wallet." He held it by a corner and shook it in front of the rabbi's face. "It contains two crisp new twenty-dollar bills, Rabbi. Now ask me what makes them so interesting."

"All right, what makes them so interesting?"

"Because up until around noon today Moose Carter didn't have a dime. He was going into Boston, and he had to borrow a couple of dollars from his mother for bus fare."

"You mean he's been selling this stuff?"

"Maybe. But what makes it really interesting is that earlier today a man was murdered in Boston, in the South End, name of Wilcox. It came over the teletype. Boston narcotics squad had been suspicious of him for some time. Just before closing time, he had cashed a check at the local branch of his bank for five hundred dollars and got it in crisp new twenties. But when you get your money in new bills, the numbers run consecutively. So when we found the grass on Moose, I called the Boston police on the chance that there might be a connection. And that's when we found out about the money. Wilcox had four hundred and sixty dollars on him when he was found, and the two bills that Moose had were the next two numbers."

"You mean that Moose murdered this Wilcox?"

"No. As a matter of fact we know that he didn't, because Wilcox was alive after Moose was seen to leave."

"Then it is definite that Moose went there?"

"The two twenty-dollar bills pretty much prove that," said Lanigan drily. "That would be proof enough for me."

"And yet, he could have got them from whoever got them from Wilcox."

"Could have but didn't. Boston has an eyewitness that saw Moose going to visit Wilcox. So you can understand why I'm not releasing the body just yet."

The rabbi nodded slowly.

"All right." Once again Lanigan was grinning, "And now ask me how we found Moose in the first place."

"Go on." For some reason the rabbi was apprehensive.

"We got a call from the next door neighbor, man named Begg, who said he had seen a light in Hillson House. So we sent the cruising car around to check it out, and they got there just in time to catch a couple of young fellows coming out. They had a car parked in front of the house, and there was a young girl behind the wheel. Now *they* might interest you, Rabbi, because one of them is the son of the president of your temple, and the other two, William Jacobs and Diane Epstein, are also your people."

# 37

"You bothered about something, lover?" asked Samantha as she sipped her coffee.

"Troubled? No. Why?"

"Well, you've been pretty quiet all evening."

"Oh, I was just wondering how Ben made out with the rabbi," said Roger Epstein. "I thought he might call and tell me about it."

"Well, they were going to her sister's in Lynn. Sarah mentioned it the other night when they were over. I suppose he just explained to him what the new policy of the temple was and told him that he expected him to go along with it."

"That's just the point. From what I've seen of him, the rabbi isn't the sort of man you can just tell what to do."

Samantha looked up from her glass.

"You mean he's stubborn?"

"No-o, not exactly stubborn. Maybe it's just that he knows just what he believes. Most people don't, you know. And he isn't the sort to do something that he believes wrong."

"But if Ben tells him —"

"All right, suppose he tells him and he refuses?"

"Well, gosh, doesn't he have to go along with Ben? Or is there some Jewish law about it? I mean, he isn't like a priest who is put in a parish by the bishop. You can ask him to leave, can't you?"

"Yes, we can. And that's what we agreed at the meeting. Ben was to spell it out for him, and if he refused to go along or if Ben decided that he wasn't going to go along — we left it up to Ben to use his judgment — why then, he was to tell him that a motion would be brought up before the board calling for his resignation." He ran his hand through his hair. "But I've been thinking about it, Sam, and I'm not so sure it was such a good idea. The way Ben explained it at the time, he could use the pulpit to help the opposition every chance he got — the Sabbath services, the community seder next week, there'll be a lot of people attending that, the holiday services the following week — besides all kinds of people who come calling on him or who he sees, like the kids yesterday, which precipitated the whole business. If we couldn't neutralize him, it would be better to fire him before he could do much damage. That was Ben's view, and we all went along with it."

"Well, it seems reasonable."

"Maybe it is, but I can't help feeling that maybe Ben exaggerated what the rabbi might do, and even more —" he hesitated.

"What?"

"I personally feel funny about it."

"How do you mean, lover?"

"Well, here I am — new to this whole game. I became a member of the temple only a few years ago, partly because Ben Gorfinkle urged me and partly because I thought, as an institution, I could use it to further the things that mean a lot to me — the Social Action Fund, for example. But I'm still only a new man. Before that, I never entered a temple from one year to the next. And here I am, one of the group who's laying down the law to the rabbi, even firing him maybe, and he's been in it all his life." He shook his head. "Well, I'm beginning to think it's damn presumptuous of me."

# 38

"All right, so it started to rain and you ran up to the house," said the rabbi, "and then what happened?"

"Well," said Bill Jacobs, "at first we tried to take shelter under the eaves — there was no porch — but it started to thunder and lightning, and the girls got frightened. It was awfully close. You can tell by how soon the thunder follows the lightning. You count —"

"I know how it's done."

"Yeah, well, so Moose suggested we go inside."

"It was Moose's suggestion? You're sure?"

"That's right," said Didi, "I remember one of the boys — I think it was Adam Sussman — asking how we were going to get in, and Moose in that very superior way of his said he'd show us. He puts the palms of his hands against the windowpane, and he sort of rotates it, and that causes the catch to loosen. Then with something thin and stiff — a little plastic ruler he had — you can stick it up between the window sashes and push it back.'' She demonstrated the technique.

''But weren't you worried about being seen?''

''Well, there's only this other house where this guy Begg lives, the one that notified the police, I understand,'' said Bill, ''and Moose was sure he wouldn't bother us.''

''Then one of you climbed in and let the others in —''

''Adam Sussman. He was the smallest and the lightest. The girls refused.''

''You are talking about the window in the rear and the back door, right?''

''That's right.''

''But you all went into the living room, which is in front of the house. Why was that?''

''We didn't want to put on a light, Rabbi, and that room got some illumination from the streetlamp across the way. Besides, I guess that was the one room that had plenty of chairs.''

''And you all stayed together in that room?''

''More or less. There was some wandering around when we first came in, and a little later a couple of people went looking for the john, but mostly we just stayed in the living room, all except Moose, of course.''

''Why do you say 'of course'?''

''Because he came back with this bottle of whisky. So I guess he'd done some exploring.''

''How much was in it? I mean, was it a full bottle?''

''Oh, it was full all right. He had to take the seal off to open it. And he offered it around first, but none of us took any, so he drank it down same as he did the beer down at the beach — showing off.''

''And then?''

''Then he started to act up.''

''What do you mean by that, Bill?''

''Oh, he was sort of chasing after the

girls, especially Betty Marks and Didi here."

"And what did the rest of you do?"

Jacobs reddened. "Well, he was pretty drunk. I mean, he couldn't catch them or anything like that, so I guess we thought it was funny. Once or twice we told him to cut it out and sit down, but most of the time we were laughing. You weren't bothered, were you, Didi?"

She shook her head.

"Then it suddenly hit him, and he got all red and just sat down. He was sweating, and he looked terrible. So I suggested he lie down for a while. I guess he thought it was a good idea, because he tried to get up. Then he just sat down again, so I helped him up, and me and Adam tried to walk him to this room I had noticed off the hall. But Moose is — was — I mean, Adam is pretty small, and Moose was a big guy. So I called to this guy Jenkins, the colored fellow, and the three of us got him into that room and laid him on the couch."

"I see."

"When we laid him down, he saw

Jenkins and he started in on him again — you know, calling him names and saying things like he didn't need no help from no goddam nigger — that kind of thing. He was throwing himself around and trying to get up. The couch had this big sheet of plastic draped over it, like the rest of the furniture, so I suggested we wrap it around him. And almost immediately he fell off to sleep."

"How do you know he was asleep?" the rabbi demanded sharply.

"Because he was snoring."

"All right. Then you went back to the living room?"

"That's right. And then Stu came along."

"And then you came back to get Moose?"

"That's right," said Bill. "We went into the room where we had left him. I had the flashlight —" He paused and licked his lips. He looked questioningly at Stu and Didi.

"Go ahead," said Stu hoarsely. "Tell it all."

# 39

"Yes, I've got a key to Hillson House," said Meyer Paff guardedly.

"And you were there this evening?" asked Lieutenant Jennings.

"I was there, but I didn't go in. Say, what's this all about?"

"There was a little trouble, and we're just checking it over," said Jennings easily. "Now, what time were you there?"

"Look, I was supposed to meet somebody at half past eight. I was a little late, and it was raining so hard I thought this party might not show. So when I got there and I saw that no one was around, I just drove on."

"Didn't it occur to you that this party you were supposed to meet might also be late? I'm surprised you didn't wait a while."

Paff shrugged. "Originally there were four of us supposed to meet. So first one calls and tells me he can't make it. And then another calls, and *he* can't make it. So I was bothered to begin with — you know, disgusted — and I half had the feeling that the third one would have begged off if he could have reached me in time. So like I said, it was raining and there was thunder and lightning, so I thought, What the hell, two of them have disappointed me, so I'll disappoint a little on my end. Good thing, too. It turns out when I got home and called him, he said he thought he had a cold coming on and wasn't about to go out in that kind of weather."

"Well, that's clear enough," said Jennings, closing his notebook. "However, just to get things cleared up, I'd appreciate it if you'd come down to the station house and make a statement."

"So what do you call this?"

"Oh, I mean a regular statement that a stenographer can take down and you can sign."

"Well . . ."

"It won't take long, maybe half an hour or so," Jennings assured him.

"All right, I'll drop by in the morning —"

"I think the chief would like to have it tonight."

"You mean right now?"

"Why not? You're dressed. I can drive you down in ten minutes, and I'll bring you back afterward."

Paff was reluctant, but he could think of no reason to refuse. "Well, all right," he said, "I'll just tell my wife, and I'll put on a pair of shoes. I don't suppose I need to wear a tie," he added with feeble humor.

"Beauty," said Jennings appreciatively.

Paff headed for the door, then stopped. "Say, what happened down there? Was the place broken into, or —?"

"Why do you think that?" asked Jennings quickly.

"Well, I understand it happened once before."

Jennings nodded. "Yeah, it was broken into again, but this time it was a little more serious. Someone was found dead there. An employee of yours, as a matter of fact," he added placidly.

# 40

"I hate to say it to a man of the cloth . . ."

"I'm not a man of the cloth."

". . . but you've got an awful nerve, Rabbi. These kids tell me they find one of their friends murdered, and you ask me to let them go."

"Why not?"

Lanigan ticked off the points on his fingers. "First, because they're guilty of breaking and entering —"

"Not Stu Gorfinkle."

"He did the second time."

"The door was ajar."

"Let's not quibble, Rabbi. So it's illegal entry. Second, they were present in the same room with someone who had narcotics in his possession."

"They didn't know that."

"The law doesn't differentiate — not here in Massachusetts, it don't. Third, they were present in the same house where a man was murdered. Fourth, they could have committed the murder. And fifth, they did not report it to the proper authorities. And you ask me to release them!" Lanigan's face was red with indignation.

"Yes, I ask you to release them," he said soberly. "These are not vagabonds; they are respectable children of respectable parents, residents of this town. If you need them for questioning, they will be available. They are obviously guilty of the breaking and entering charge — they admit it, even though it's fully understandable in view of the storm. Still, if you should decide to prosecute them on that charge, they will appear. As for the narcotics charge, it is based on a law which obviously was never intended to be taken literally — would you arrest everyone on a streetcar, for example, if one passenger was carrying narcotics? No, it is intended to enable you to prosecute someone you have reason to believe is involved in narcotics, even though the actual possession may be with a companion. Are you suggesting that while they were waiting for transportation home they were smoking this drug?"

"And the murder?"

"That they didn't report it immediately — that was wrong of them but I think understandable. They're youngsters, and they were worried about what they should do. They were aware that suspicion could fall on them, and they wanted to discuss it among themselves — not whether to report it or not, but how. If you honestly think that one of them, or all of them, were actually involved in the murder, then again, they will be available for questioning." He smiled. "In the past, you have been receptive to suggestions that I have made that are based on Talmudic law —"

"You going to try to hornswoggle me with that pil — what do you call it?"

"Pilpul? No, but there is the principle of *miggo.*"

"I don't think you ever tried that one on me before. How does it go?" asked

293

Lanigan, interested in spite of himself.

"You might call it a principle of inferring credibility. The rabbi would use it when sitting in judgment. It is based on the general psychological principle that a man will not plead to a greater crime if a lesser or more advantageous plea is available to him, for 'the mouth that bound is the mouth that loosed.' "

"I don't get it."

"Let me give you a classic example. A marriageable woman coming from a distant land to a place where she is not known says that although she had been married, she is now divorced and free to marry again. She is to be believed both as to the marriage and the divorce, since she could easily have said that she had never been married at all and have no questions raised about her status."

"All right, and how does it apply here?"

"Once the youngsters unwrapped the body, there was no evidence that a murder had been committed. They could have remained silent, and you would have assumed that it was a natural death. After all, there were no marks visible on the body. But they made no attempt to conceal what they found. They told you, and so I say that under the principle of *miggo,* they are to be believed both on their testimony and on their innocence."

Lanigan rose from his chair and paced the floor while the rabbi maintained a watchful silence. Finally, he stepped in front of the rabbi and spread his hands in exasperation. "What do you want me to do, Rabbi? I called their parents and not one of them was home. The girl says her folks are at a movie; she doesn't even know which one. You want me to call all the local movie houses and have them paged? That Gorfinkle boy, he finally told me his folks were at his aunt's house, but when I called, they had left. And Mr. and Mrs. Jacobs — why, they're in Boston at some party. He doesn't know the name of the people — or he says he doesn't. You know I can't let them go until I get hold of their parents. They're minors."

"You'll be better off to let them go home. If you wait until their parents get here, this place will be a madhouse of hysterical parents and whatever lawyers they managed to bring along with them. There will be accusations and recriminations, and worst of all, the town will be full of rumors tomorrow morning that not only will do a great deal of harm to a lot of innocent people, but will make your investigation ten times as complicated and ten times as difficult."

Lanigan shook his head stubbornly. "If one of those kids turned out to be guilty and I let him get away when I had him right here in my own station house —" He broke off to ask a patrolman who had entered and was trying to catch his eye, "What is it, Tony?"

"Can I talk to you for a minute, Chief?" The two withdrew to a corner of the room, where the patrolman whispered to him earnestly for several minutes. The chief asked him a question and got a muttered reply. Then, with a "Thanks, Tony, that's a real help," he rejoined the rabbi.

"All right, Rabbi, I'll tell you what I'll do: I'll release them in your custody. You'll have to give me your word that they'll be available for questioning when I want them."

For a moment the rabbi hesitated. Then he nodded. "Very well, I guess I can do that."

# 41

They had been there almost an hour, and still there was no sign of agreement. Every now and then one of them would appeal to the rabbi — usually to support his position — but he was determined to be circumspect and refused to be drawn. When Lanigan first asked him to arrange for an informal meeting with all the youngsters who had been at the cookout, he had demurred. "I can't just ask them; their parents would have to agree to it."

"So ask the parents. Explain to them that all I want is information. I'm not trying to pin anything on anyone. No tricks. I just want to be sure I'm getting the complete story."

"They'll want their lawyers present," the rabbi warned.

"Nothing doing. I'm not going to have

a bunch of wise guys raising objections every time I ask a question. If one didn't, another would."

"How about if they all agreed on one lawyer?"

"That would be the day. Besides, even if by some miracle they did, he'd feel he had to be extra careful, and he wouldn't let them volunteer anything."

The rabbi smiled. "Then I don't think you're going to get your meeting."

"Oh, I'll get it sooner or later," said Lanigan grimly. "I've got a clear case of breaking and entering against each and every one of those kids. I'll admit that there were extenuating circumstances and that probably no judge would sentence them. But in connection with the fact that they were all material witnesses to a murder — believe me, I'd have no trouble confining them to the jurisdiction. And when school starts again, they and their parents, too, are going to begin to chafe."

So, with great reluctance, the rabbi had agreed and called Mr. Jacobs to ask him to round up the others.

They met in his study, and after his

preliminary remarks explaining the situation, he left the entire discussion to them. He sat teetering in his swivel chair behind his desk, following the argument as it shifted back and forth among the parents. Gorfinkle, for once, remained uncharacteristically silent, and the rabbi for his part tended to avoid looking in his direction.

"If he's going to accuse *my* child of being mixed up in the murder of this — this football player, then he's going to have to prove it," cried Betty Marks' mother. "The nerve of him to expect *me* to permit *him* to question *her* without a lawyer."

"I'm sure he doesn't suspect her, Mrs. Marks," said Roger Epstein. "He just wants to clear this business up as fast as he can. If we don't cooperate, he'll get nowhere, sure, but the case will not be solved."

"Well, that's his lookout," said Mrs. Marks.

"No, it's ours, too. If the case isn't solved and the murderer found, after a while suspicion may rest on our children, and that won't do any of them any good."

"Besides," said Mr. Schulman, "the kids did break into that house. No question about it. If we don't cooperate in this, he can bring a charge on the grounds of breaking and entering. Well, my Gladys has to get back to school; she has exams just as soon as she gets back. Am I going to let her kill a year just to be stubborn? Anyway, I trust my Gladys."

"Do you mean I don't trust my Betty?"

"I'm sure you have every reason to, Mrs. Marks," said Epstein quickly.

"I think Bill should be able to handle himself," said Mr. Jacobs. "I'm willing to go along."

"Yes, but Bill was one of those who discovered the body," said Mr. Sussman. "His situation and your Stu's, Ben, they're different."

"I don't see that they're so different," said Gorfinkle. "After all, Stu never even entered the house until they went back for the other boy."

"You mean he's in the clear, and that's why you're so willing," Mr.

Sussman pointed out.

"We'll be here all night if we keep on wrangling like this," said Mr. Arons. "What's it come down to? Chief Lanigan wants to question our kids all together on an informal basis. He's certainly got a right to question them, and we've got a right to have a lawyer present. So if he questions them individually, don't you think he'll get the answers to any questions he wants to ask even if there is a lawyer present? If he doesn't get it from one, he'll get it from another. You know, folks, I get the impression that this Lanigan is a sincere guy. I think he's on the level. I don't think he's trying to trap anybody."

"It just occurred to me," said Mr. Sussman. "If there's no lawyer present, then none of what is said can be used as evidence in court. So maybe we're better off without a lawyer."

"That's a good point," said Schulman.

"That's right. Maybe Lanigan outsmarted himself."

"I still think one of us ought to be present, though."

"I don't know how Lanigan would feel about that," said Jacobs. "Personally, I wouldn't care to be the one. I wouldn't care to be responsible to the rest of you for advising your kids. Suppose one of them said something damaging —"

"Suppose we got someone who is not involved, someone neutral," Epstein offered.

"Like who?"

"Perhaps" — Mr. Arons turned — "the rabbi here —"

# 42

Lieutenant Jennings glanced through the typed sheets and handed them over to his chief. "There's Paff's statement, Hugh. Nothing very interesting in it, although it struck me that he was kind of edgy."

"Everybody's edgy when they have to talk to the police," said Lanigan. "That's one of the troubles with being a cop." He read from the statement: " 'QUESTION: What is your interest in Hillson House? ANSWER: I'm thinking of buying it; that is, a group of us are. QUESTION: For what purpose? ANSWER: It's a business venture.' " Lanigan looked up. "He never told you what it was?"

"No, Hugh, he acted pretty closed-mouthed about it, and I didn't feel I had the right to pry, especially when I couldn't see any connection. After all, if it's some special deal, he naturally wouldn't want it to get out before he was ready."

"Maybe you're right. But did he say who the group was?"

"Yeah, later on he mentions at least some of the names. There's a guy name of Arons who is the father of one of the kids, and there's Dr. Edelstein — you know him — and there's a man name of Kallen, Irving Kallen. He was supposed to meet them at the site, but none of them showed, so he drove off."

"That's a little funny," said Lanigan. "If he got there early, you'd think he'd wait. And if he got there late, he might assume that someone else could be late, and you'd think he'd wait for a few minutes anyway."

"Not if you read the statement, Hugh. Edelstein and Arons called earlier to tell him they wouldn't make it. It was raining so hard he figured Kallen wouldn't come out either." He leaned over and pointed to a paragraph on the typescript. " 'I slowed down, saw that no one was there and the house was dark, and drove on.' "

"Hm — maybe. But still, there's the business of his bowling alleys —"

"Gosh, Hugh, bowling is respectable these days. Some alleys have these little tables where you have a bite, and there are even some where women can bring the kids and leave them with a baby-sitter while they bowl. Pool and billiard parlors, the same way. You know that one over at the shopping center? I dropped in there one evening while the missus was shopping in the supermarket, and there was this gal in a miniskirt stretched out on that table making a shot for the corner pocket. You could see her whole whatsis. I tell you, I just had to get up and leave."

"I'll bet."

Jennings disregarded his chief's sarcasm. "Say, do you suppose that's the deal on Hillson House? He and his friends want to turn it into one of them fancy bowling alleys?"

"Could be. Still, it's funny about him."

"What's funny?"

"Well, there's that call from Kevin O'Connor. Kevin is an idiot, but he's also a cop. He wouldn't go asking me about

306

Paff just to gossip. I take it that the Lynn police are really suspicious of that bowling alley of his. Anyway, it's a coincidence. And his having a key to Hillson House is another. And his driving by there that same night — that's still another. It's a lot of coincidences when you come to think of it.''

''Yeah, but he's a big man in the community. What could the likes of him have to do with the likes of Moose Carter?''

''Well, for one thing, Moose worked for him.''

''So?''

''So it's a connection. Suppose, just suppose,'' said Lanigan slowly, ''Paff were distributing pot. Remember, a lot of kids come into his bowling alleys. Now suppose, just suppose, that after working there for a while, Moose tumbles onto it. You know the sort of kid he was. He wouldn't notify the police. Oh no, he'd tell Paff and make him cough up for it. All right, Paff goes to Hillson House for this special deal. When his friends don't show, he figures while he's there he might as well look the place over again. He goes from room to room, and then he sees Moose. Maybe so far the kid only hit him up for small change. Maybe for that package of pot we found on him. But he knows it's not going to stop there. It's going to get worse. And then he realizes that he can settle the whole business by just lifting up a corner of the sheet and tucking it in."

"You mean he'd kill him to avoid being blackmailed? Seems to me he'd be more apt to wait until the kid actually bore down on him."

"Maybe he did. Or look at it this way: Maybe he wouldn't go out of his way to do anything drastic, but here an opportunity presents itself. All he has to do it tuck in a fold of plastic and walk away."

"Beauty! But you've got to admit, Hugh, that it's pretty fanciful. I wouldn't want to put the arm on anybody on the basis of that kind of evidence."

"Oh, I'm keeping an open mind on the subject. I haven't written off those kids by a long shot. Remember, they all knew

Moose. Any one of them could have done it, girls as well as boys. Maybe some of those girls were sweet on some of the boys and vice versa. And from what I can gather, Moose was cracking wise quite a bit. We know he fooled around with the girls, and maybe someone there didn't like it. So when he passed out —"

"All right, so now you've got the eight kids — no, seven, because the Gorfinkle boy wasn't there. Are you sure you can't get him involved?"

Lanigan disregarded Jennings' sarcasm. "No, I can't come up with anything for him. I'd say he was in the clear."

"Then I'll give you one. How about old man Carter?"

"Carter, the boy's father?"

"Stepfather, Hugh."

"That's right. I forgot about that. What difference does it make, though? He adopted him, I suppose. Anyway he brought him up as his own. Who *was* the boy's father?"

Jennings grinned. "He was born over the left. He wasn't Carter's boy, that's for sure. And the old man could never forget it. Whenever he had trouble with him, and there was trouble with the police once or twice, he blamed it on the boy's birth. He told me once when Moose was involved on a matter of vandalism that it was because he was a child of sin and came of bad seed."

"Pretty rotten that."

"Oh, it's what you'd expect from these religious types. Well, now, that night Carter wasn't home. When we called, he was just coming in."

"I suppose it might be worthwhile knowing where he was," Lanigan admitted with no great interest. "Anyone else?"

"There's the colored fellow, of course."

"Well, naturally. He's probably the one. Still, no harm in checking over the possibles."

# 43

The manager of the Lynn alleys greeted Paff with, "Tough about the kid, huh?"

Paff shook his head regretfully. "It certainly is. A young fellow like that, a good-looking boy, an athlete —"

"You know, I called his house like you told me, to see why he hadn't showed, and I spoke to his Ma. When I think that he was probably dead at the time — you know, it kind of gives you the shivers — I mean asking her what time she expects him back and all."

"Yeah."

"You got somebody else lined up to take his place, Mr. Paff? Because life got to go on, like they say, and I don't mind working overtime a couple of nights to help you out, but —"

"I'll get somebody to relieve you —

tomorrow night for sure."

"If you're having trouble getting somebody, there's this kid that lives right next door to me. He's smart, knows how to handle himself."

"Yeah? What's he doing now?"

"Well, right now, he's not doing much of anything, just sort of looking around."

"Well —"

"I could have him come down tomorrow evening, and you could talk to him."

"Right now, I've got things pretty well lined up."

A customer tapped impatiently on the counter with a coin, and the manager hurried over to wait on him. As he came back he fished in his pocket and brought forth a bit of paper. "Say, I almost forgot. Did a Mr. Kallen get in touch with you the other night? He called right after you left. He said he was supposed to meet you" — he referred to the paper — "at Hillson House. He said he wouldn't be able to make it. Say, wasn't that the place that —"

"Yeah, I spoke to him. Look, er —" he

nodded him down to the other end of the counter. "The other night I was kind of upset. I had a tough day, understand?"

"Sure, Mr. Paff. We all have them."

"Well, in case anybody comes down to make inquiries — not likely to, you understand, but just in case — I'd rather you wouldn't mention I was planning to fire the kid. They might get the wrong impression." He laughed — a deep bass burble. "Hell, I wouldn't have fired him, not a kid from my hometown."

"Sure, Mr. Paff. What they don't know won't hurt them."

"I want you to cooperate with them, understand? Tell them everything, but there's no need to tell them anything unimportant. Now if they should ask when I left here, you remember it was sometime after eight o'clock —"

"Oh, no, Mr. Paff, it was quite a bit before —"

"No, it was after, almost quarter past. This friend of yours — you think he'd work out?"

"Oh, he's smart, Mr. Paff."

"All right, I guess you're a pretty good

313

judge of character. Tell him to come down tomorrow night, and I'll put him on."

"Gee, thanks, Mr. Paff. You leave him to me, and I'll show him the ropes. You won't be sorry."

# 44

Chief Lanigan knew that the youngsters in his living room were there by coercion and that if he tried to appear friendly, they would only mistrust him more. So he tried candor.

"I won't ask you to make yourselves comfortable because I know you can't until this business is cleared up. That would be asking a lot. But there's coffee here and some cookies and for those who want something cold, Coke. Help yourselves."

"I'll have a cup of coffee," said Adam Sussman.

"So will I," said Bill Jacobs.

"I'd like a Coke, please," said Betty Marks.

Chief Lanigan, with the rabbi helping, passed out drinks and cookies. Then, when they were settled, he began again. "All of you participated in a cookout on the beach at Tarlow's Point last Monday evening —"

"Just a minute," said Jacobs. "There was someone else."

"You're referring to Alan Jenkins?"

"That's right."

"I asked the Boston police to contact him for us. He lives in a boarding house and his landlady said he had gone off to New York. We have also contacted the New York police and asked them to look him up for us. In the meantime I'm afraid we'll have to do without him. Now, sometime during the evening you were joined by Moose Carter. And a little while later Gorfinkle here had to leave to pick up his folks, thus leaving you without transportation when the storm started. You ran for cover to Hillson House, forced a window, and took shelter inside."

"Just a minute," said Adam Sussman. "I'm not admitting anything."

Lanigan sighed. "Let's get one thing straight, Sussman: I'm not trying to trap

316

you. Everything I have said and everything I'm going to say I can prove easily. I'm just trying to find out what happened. The point I was trying to make is that you were all guilty of breaking and entering. Under the circumstances, your behavior has some justification. That was a pretty frightening storm. What's more, it seems that you did nothing but take shelter. There is no evidence of vandalism, and as far as we can make out, nothing was taken. But it was breaking and entering, and I can hold you for it." He looked around at them pointedly.

"That's blackmail, isn't it?" said Jacobs.

"Yes," said Lanigan pleasantly.

"So what do you want to know?"

"Let's start from the beginning."

"All right, so you, Jacobs, and Sussman marched him into the study," said Lanigan. "Just a minute." He went to the hall closet and came back with a package. "I stopped off at the hardware store earlier and got one of those plastic drop cloths. It's just about the size of the plastic dust cover in the study at Hillson House." He unfolded it and spread it on the floor. "Now, Gorfinkle, suppose you lie down on that, and Jacobs can show us how he wrapped Moose."

Stu lay down on the sheet as everyone craned forward to watch. But Bill Jacobs shook his head. "The sheet was draped sort of catty-cornered on the couch, so that Moose was lying on the diagonal. Move your carcass around, Stu. That's right." Suiting the action to the words, he proceeded to demonstrate. "First, we picked up this corner and covered his feet. Then we picked up this corner and wrapped it tight around his body and kind of tucked it in. Then we picked up the opposite corner and wrapped it over that and tucked it under him, like this."

"And was anything said at the time, or had Moose passed out?"

"No, he was swearing, mostly at Jenkins."

"And Jenkins, did he say anything?"

"Not that I remember, except when we finished wrapping him up and he fell asleep, Jenkins said — but it was just in fun —"

"What did he say?"

"Oh, something about we ought to put it over his flippin' head." And then Jacobs added quickly, "But he was just joking."

"Of course," said Lanigan easily. "Now, when you came back to Hillson House, how did you find Moose? Any change in the way he was wrapped?"

"Well, this top corner had been pulled over and tucked in where the folds of the plastic met."

"Show me."

"Hey!" from Stu.

"Don't worry, Gorfinkle, we won't leave you there," Lanigan reassured him.

Bill Jacobs lifted the upper corner of the sheet and folded it over Stu's head and tucked it in.

Sue Arons shrieked. "Take it off," she cried hysterically, "take it off!"

# 45

In company Pearl Jacobs was gay, almost giddy, but in the privacy of her home, with her family, she could be sober and shrewd. When her husband had finished describing the meeting of the parents at the rabbi's study, she said, ''I don't understand why the rabbi called you. I should think it would be Gorfinkle he'd call. He's the president.''

''He said it was because our Bill was the only one who had been involved with the affair from beginning to end, but of course, his real reason was that he was probably embarrassed about calling Ben Gorfinkle after he had threatened to give him the ax.''

''I'll bet Ben wouldn't be elected now if he were to run.''

''Why? Because he ticked off the rabbi?

You think *he's* so popular?"

"No. I mean, I don't know how popular the rabbi is. I know he doesn't have a special following. And some of those parents may feel sore at him for getting the kids to tell the police what they knew."

"You think so?"

She nodded. "I felt that way myself when I first heard of it, but then I realized it was bound to come out sooner or later. Besides, I didn't like the idea of a murderer running around loose and —"

"What's that got to do with Ben Gorfinkle?" said her husband patiently.

She looked at him in surprise. "Simply that a lot of the girls feel that this fight in the congregation he started is not such a good idea."

"Yes, but the girls don't vote."

"Maybe no," she said, "but a lot of them can influence those who do vote. And in Reform congregations they do vote, and I think it's a good idea. Anyway, a lot of the women I talked to, they don't like the idea of building an organization like this and then breaking it in two over a silly business of who is to sit where."

"Look, Pearl, I hope you don't talk that way outside. We weren't trying to split the organization. And it isn't over the seating business; that's just incidental. We have a program and a damn good program, and at every step of the way we were blocked by Paff and his group. Since we can't get them to agree, wouldn't it be better if the two views, the two philosophies, should each have their own machinery for doing what they consider important, instead of each preventing the other from doing anything?"

"Isn't that just like a man?" She shook her head. "You say we don't want to split; we just want to do the things that cause a split. And that satisfies your conscience. Well, let me tell you that women are a lot more realistic. You're like a bunch of kids who think if you don't give it a name, it doesn't exist. But you know what a split does? It isn't just that you get two temples where you only had one before. It means that you get two groups that tend to keep away from each other. The people of one temple tend to stay away from the people of the other temple. It doesn't make so much difference to the men — they're away all day, and most evenings they're too tired to do anything. But the women are around here all day long. Take me and Marjie Arons; we're both in Women's League. And we're close. All right, the temple splits, and I'm in one temple and Marjie is in the other. Don't you think that will put up a wall between us?"

"But we don't see them socially, anyway," he protested.

"We don't as a couple see them as a couple, because you don't like him, and I'm not crazy about him either. But Marjie and I see each other. And how about the kids?"

"What about them?" he asked.

"Well, if there are two temples, there will be different affairs, and the kids from one temple will feel funny about going to affairs from the other place. Here's Bill out in this dinky little college in a town in Minnesota that nobody has ever heard of. From ·what he tells me, there are less than a dozen Jewish families in the whole town and practically no eligible Jewish girls. Do you think that doesn't worry me? But at least when he comes home for his vacations here, there are plenty of Jewish girls. He can play the field. And you now want to cut off half of them. Do you want your son to marry a Gentile, God forbid?"

"Come on, Pearl, you're making a big deal — do you think if Bill wants to take a girl out, he's going to bother about what temple her folks go to?"

"No," she said, "but he'll have less chance of meeting them."

"Well, a temple is not a matrimonial bureau."

"There are lots worse things that it could be, especially in a Yankee town like Barnard's Crossing. Why do you suppose the Sisterhood works so hard to make a go of it? You think it's so that you men can go there two or three times a year to mumble your prayers? We put on bazaars, and we put on shows. We have luncheons and brunches and whatnot. We have a big educational program. And at the end of the year, we hand the temple organization a whopping big check. We do it, I suppose, because some of it is fun and keeps us busy. But Marjie Arons does it partly to increase the chances of her Sue marrying a Jewish boy, and I do it to help insure that Bill marries a Jewish girl."

"The rabbi —"

"He doesn't know any more about it than you do. He's a man, too. I'll bet the *rebbitzin* understand though."

"I see," Jacobs said with a laugh. "And how long have you girls been plotting? When do you plan to take over?"

"Who needs it? You men want to run things? Go ahead. Big shots! You're like kids with a toy. You play with it, and then you get tired of it and leave it lying around or break it. You go ahead and plan and appoint committees, take votes, pass resolutions, make — what did Ben Gorfinkle call it? — 'an active voice for social reform in the community' or what the rabbi is always talking about, 'a house of study and prayer' — but don't break it. Because it isn't only for you; it's for us —

and for the kids."

"I see, so the kids are in on it, too?" he asked sarcastically.

"Don't run down the kids. Sometimes they show more sense than their parents. Our Bill is no fool. He was talking to me about it. He was concerned that the rabbi might leave. Now the kids like him and respect him. That's why Bill told the police — because the rabbi said he ought to, and Bill trusted him."

"Does Mrs. Paff think the way you do?"

"She has no children, so she doesn't feel about these things the way I do, I suppose. But Paff himself — if I were in his business that depends so much on kids, I wouldn't go out of my way to antagonize them."

# 46

"Well, what do you think?" asked Lanigan.

"I don't think you learned too much, did you?" the rabbi countered. "Still, there were a number of points brought out that I thought interesting. They seemed quite unanimously agreed that it was the Carter boy who first suggested that they invade Hillson House and who assured them that they would not be seen."

Lanigan grinned. "Sure, it was safe to blame him; he can't answer back."

"There is that, of course —"

"I found that little dig by the Epstein girl about the Marks girl having dated Moose quite a bit last year interesting."

"You attribute any significance to that? You didn't pursue it at the time."

"I thought it would be more profitable

to inquire about it later on."

"Really? I regarded it as normal female cattiness," observed the rabbi. "About the only other bit of evidence I found worthwhile was the matter of the front door."

"What was that?"

"Bill Jacobs saying that he remembered fixing the latch on the front door so that they could come back and get Moose."

"Oh yes," said Lanigan. "Why do you regard that as especially important?"

"Because it means that after they left, anyone could have got in."

"If they had known," Lanigan interjected swiftly. "But it wouldn't have made any difference to someone with a key."

"Like who?"

"Like a man named Paff. Know him? He's a member of your temple."

"Meyer Paff?"

"That's right. He had a key to the place and was around there that night at about the right time."

Rabbi Small did not answer immediately. "Look here," he said at last, "obviously there's much about this case I don't know. There's no reason for me to know it. It's police business. But if it concerns members of my congregation and you want me to cooperate —"

"Keep your shirt on, Rabbi. I was planning to give it all to you." He went to the hall closet and returned with an attaché case. "Here's a copy of Paff's statement."

The rabbi read it through and then looked up and said mildly, "It seems straightforward enough."

"Oh, it is," said Lanigan hastily. "And yet, there are some interesting aspects to the very fact that he was there. For one thing, he knew the boy. Moose worked for him."

"Mr. Paff is an active member of the Boosters Club here in town and knows most of the high school athletes. He would certainly know Moose Carter."

"It's just a little detail. Here's another: The Lynn bowling alley has been under the surveillance of the Lynn police. They suspect it of being a distribution point for pot. Paff owns it, and that was where

Moose used to work evenings as an assistant manager."

"Are you suggesting that Moose did the distributing and that Paff killed him for it?"

"That's a possibility," said Lanigan judiciously.

"Almost anything is," said the rabbi with a shrug. "But I doubt if you're really serious about Mr. Paff —"

"No, and why not?"

"Well, for one thing, I don't think you would have gone to the trouble of rounding up these youngsters and questioning them all evening."

"That's for sure," he grinned. "But unlike you, Rabbi, I found this meeting with the kids very enlightening."

"Indeed!"

"In fact, it practically proved what I've suspected all along, but I had to have this meeting to confirm it. A definite pattern developed — and it all points unmistakably to Jenkins."

"Oh?"

"Yes, it started when Moose first joined the group. He began to ride Jenkins, and there is no doubt from what the kids said that the colored fellow was burning about it. They were all in agreement on that."

"But Jenkins didn't do anything about it. None of them reported him as saying anything," the rabbi observed.

"No, and he didn't come out swinging at any time either. Maybe it would have been better if he had. That kind of thing builds up. He doesn't say anything until Moose is being wrapped up in the sheet. Then he cracks they ought to put it over his head. The Jacobs boy said he was joking, but you know that a lot of jokes — things that just pop out — are meant seriously."

"Go on."

"Next point: Jacobs leaves the door off the latch. Now who knows that? Why, only Jacobs. You remember I questioned him on that rather closely. He was the last one out, and he set the latch. Now later, when they were in the Epstein house and were planning to go back for Moose, Gorfinkle asked how they were going to get in and it was *then* that Jacobs told the others that he had set the latch so that it

331

wouldn't lock. It's the usual front-door lock with two buttons. One releases the latch, and the other locks it. And notice, that's when Jenkins said he had to be getting right home because he was setting out for New York the next morning early.''

"And you think he rode off and on the way to Boston stopped off at Hillson House.''

"I'm damn sure of it. He had the opportunity; that is, he had transportation — his motorbike. And he had the motive. He's the only one we know definitely had a motive.''

"Because young Carter made fun of him? Did it ever occur to you that Jenkins might be used to this kind of embarrassment? That this incident probably was merely another of a long series of similar incidents he has had to suffer all his life?''

"You mean you can get used to it. Sure, but it can also build up. And this could have been the last straw. You can argue these things either way. I should think you'd be happy over the turn of events."

"Happy? Happy that a young man who has visited in my house however briefly is suspected of murder?"

"Come on, Rabbi. Let's be practical. Moose Carter was murdered, and that means that somebody murdered him. Now who are the suspects? Well, up till now it has been the kids from your congregation and Meyer Paff, another of your people. I should think that you'd be happy that it's not them, that it's not somebody you're closely associated with, that it's somebody from out of town, a stranger."

"Ah, the stranger. Thank God for the stranger."

The rabbi rose from his chair and began striding back and forth across the room. "We Jews celebrate the Passover in a couple of days. In many respects it's a most unique holiday, and we celebrate it in a unique way. We begin by cleaning the house of all foods and even all utensils that we use during the year, and during the week of the festival we not only buy special foods, but prepare them in special utensils and eat them from special dishes

333

with special silverware that are used for just that week. Then on the eve of the holiday we have a feast, which is repeated the following night. And in each case the feast is preceded by an elaborate ritual in which the youngest person present asks the meaning of the feast, of the unusual foods that we eat, and the unusual manner of eating them. And then we, the rest of the company, explain how we were slaves in Egypt and were oppressed and how God responded to our suffering by bringing us forth with a mighty hand from our slavery and oppression."

"Yes, Rabbi, I know the reason for the holiday. But what's the point?"

"The point is that Passover is not merely a holiday of thanksgiving or rejoicing. We have several such holidays, but this is the only one that has a very elaborate and specific ritual and involves the use of a special set of instructions, the Haggadah, to make sure we follow it exactly right. Why?"

"Tell me."

"To engrave the lessons it teaches on our minds," said the rabbi. "It's a mnemonic, a string around the finger, a way of forcing on our consciousness and memory what people would rather not think of or would easily forget.''

''Once a year the Pope washes and kisses the feet of beggars,'' Lanigan said.

''Precisely. And no doubt he profits by the lesson in humility that it teaches him,'' said the rabbi primly. Then he added as an afterthought, ''It's a pity it isn't required of all members of your faith.''

Lanigan laughed. ''All right, Rabbi. Now what is it that your holiday teaches?''

''It is associated with a specific commandment that is central in our law: 'And if a stranger sojourn with thee in your land, ye shall not do him wrong . . . he shall be as the homeborn among you; for ye were strangers in the land of Egypt.' ''

''You saying that I'm being unfair to Jenkins because he's colored and from out of town?''

''Do you have him in custody, and has he confessed?''

''We haven't got him yet, Rabbi, but

we'll get him. It's that motorbike of his — it's not like a car. You can wheel one of those over the sidewalk into a hallway or even a cellar, and how is it to be found? But I have alerted the New York police, and they'll find him."

"But you don't have any real evidence against him — only what you consider his motive and the opportunity."

"Oh, we've got the evidence, all right," said Lanigan. "We had it that first night, which is why I let your young people go home. As soon as the youngsters told us what they found and we knew it was murder, I sent some of my men scouring around Hillson House to see what they could pick up. And right off the bat, we got it. There's a tall, thick hedge in front of the house, and behind it, in the soft earth where it would be hidden from the street, we found a perfect motorbike tire mark."

# 47

The carpenter entered diffidently, awkwardly doffed his old-fashioned, wide-brimmed felt hat, and in response to the rabbi's invitation, sat down on the edge of the chair. "My wife thought I ought to change," he said in explanation of the black suit he was wearing, the highly polished black shoes, the white shirt, its collar uncomfortably tight, the wide florid necktie. "Out of respect, you know."

The rabbi nodded, not because he understood, but as a sign for him to go on.

"Lanigan called me this morning to tell me to come down to make arrangements for the burial. He said they had decided that they didn't need an autopsy."

"I see."

"So after I made the arrangements, I

337

thought I'd stop off and thank you."

"I did nothing, Mr. Carter. Nothing."

"Well, I figure if you hadn't gone down Monday night —"

"No, Mr. Carter," said the rabbi firmly, "that really had nothing to do with it, Chief Lanigan quite properly refused to release the body then because he had doubts about the cause of death. Quite rightly, as it turned out. When he discovered that the death was by asphyxiation, he consulted with the Medical Examiner, who told him that an autopsy was unnecessary and that they would learn nothing by it. As I understand it, acute alcohol poisoning results in a paralysis of the nerve that controls breathing, so that the effect on the organs is the same as asphyxiation."

"I still think that if you hadn't gone down there they might have gone through with it anyway. Doctors have been known to do it, you know, just for practice," he added darkly.

"You've made plans for the funeral?" asked the rabbi to get him off the subject.

Carter nodded. "We're having a private

affair — just the family. We didn't want a crowd, so it's just the family and a preacher friend of mine that I worked with on the fluoridation campaign. He'll say a few words."

"I think that's best."

"You know, Rabbi, I might have saved that boy." Carter clenched his fists. "I wouldn't say it to my wife, but I'm telling you."

"How do you mean?"

"I didn't listen, Rabbi. The Lord spoke to me, and I didn't listen."

The rabbi looked up with interest. "Oh?"

"I went out looking for him that night. I looked downtown and looked in the taverns, because that's where I thought I might find him. And when he wasn't there, I just rode around, up one street and down the other, aimless-like. I rode up by Tarlow's Point. Now why did I go up there if the Lord wasn't directing me? I even slowed down as I passed Hillson House. Was the Lord directing my footsteps or wasn't He?" he demanded. "But I was angry with the lad, and it blocked out the voice of the Lord. If I had been receptive, He would have spoken to me and told me where to look. But my mind was blocked, Rabbi, and the voice couldn't come through.''

''You mustn't think that way, Mr. Carter.''

''I feel better for having unburdened myself, Rabbi. I had to say it to someone, and I just couldn't say it to my wife. Oh I know the Lord moves in mysterious ways, and it's part of some great plan that's beyond the capacity of my mind or else it's punishment on me or maybe even on my wife for sins committed in the past. But I want you to know that my own faith hasn't wavered — not for a moment. And if my anger blocked out the voice, maybe that was part of the divine plan, too. Or maybe it was to teach me that my anger was a wickedness.''

''Are you suggesting the Lord would take your son's life just to teach you to control your anger?'' asked the rabbi sharply.

''I don't know, but it is the duty of His servants to try to understand Him. And why else did the thought come to my head?"

"Not all the thoughts that come to a man's head, Mr. Carter, are put there by God. And not all the things that happen are God's work. If you see His hand in everything that happens, after a while you'll begin blaming Him for unpleasant and wicked things that happen. Some things are the results of our own mistakes, and some things just happen by accident."

Carter rose. "I don't like to hear you say that, Rabbi. It seems to me that it shows a lack of faith, and I didn't expect it of you. But maybe you're just saying it to make me feel better." He rose and went to the door. He seemed hurt.

"You'll find, Rabbi," he said, and he patted him on the arm, "that if you have faith, everything comes out right in the end." He brightened and his face even relaxed in a grin. "By the by, they've caught that colored fellow that took my boy's life. They were bringing him in when I was down the station."

Carter left, and the rabbi turned to Miriam. "Where's my coat?" he said, "I'm going down to the station house."

# 48

Ben Gorfinkle had called up in midmorning to say that he was coming home for lunch. "I want to talk to Stu. He hasn't gone out, has he?"

"He's still in bed, Ben," said his wife.

"It's eleven o'clock. Do you think perhaps he might condescend to get up by noon so that I can have a few words with him?"

"Well, you kept him up so late last night quizzing him about the meeting."

"I stayed up just as late, didn't I? It didn't prevent me from getting up at a reasonable hour."

"Well, he's a young boy, and they need more sleep. Is anything the matter?"

"I just want to talk to him. You just make sure that he stays there until I get home."

He had finished his Spartan lunch of a sandwich and coffee by the time Stu, yawning and gaping, appeared in pajamas and bathrobe.

"What's up, Dad?"

"If you'd been up, you might have got the news on the radio. This Jenkins fellow — he's been taken into custody."

"Oh yeah? So?"

"I've talked to one of our lawyers down at the plant. He thinks it was a mistake on our part to let Lanigan quiz you without the protection of a lawyer present."

"Well, natch, he's a lawyer. What else is he going to say?"

The elder Gorfinkle gave his son a mental mark for shrewdness. "Anyway, he agreed with me that your case is entirely different from that of the others, and if you play your cards right, you don't have to get involved at all." Seeing his son was about to object, he plunged on. "Now, listen to me, will you? There are just three things, three hurdles that we've got to get over. First, there's the business of holding the picnic on Tarlow's Point. If that's a private beach, then you

344

were trespassing. As far as I can make out, you had nothing to do with deciding to hold the cookout there, but on the other hand, you did the driving. Then again, as I understand it, even the town counsel isn't sure whether that's a private beach or not. It's my opinion that you're perfectly safe in admitting that you knew you were going to the Point. You just say that you thought it was a public beach because there have been cookouts there before.''

''Well, sure —''

''Just listen, will you! All right. You left before the storm, and you had nothing to do with breaking into Hillson House. Right? And when you came back — the first time, I mean — you didn't go in, did you?''

Stu shook his head, wondering what his father was getting at.

''You heard them inside, and so you called out that you had come back, and they opened the door. Right?''

''Well, I knocked —''

''But you heard them in there. That's why you knocked. To let them know you had come back. And you yourself didn't go in. That's right, isn't it? You didn't go in."

"Yeah, they came out."

"All right. So far, you're in the clear. You were just like a bus driver or a cab driver who delivers a bunch of people to a party and then comes back for them. Now, when you returned to get that boy, Moose, that's when you made a mistake, because you had no right to enter that house. One thing in your favor, of course, is that the door was open, so it was not breaking and entering. And get this. All the time you were thinking that there was this friend of yours lying sick, maybe seriously sick, in that house there —"

"You mean Moose? He was no friend of mine."

"He was a classmate, wasn't he? You never had a fight with him, did you? All right, so he was a friend of yours. And he was sick —"

"He was drunk."

"You didn't know that. All you knew was that they told you he had passed out. That's like fainted. That's serious. You had a car, so naturally you felt you had to go help him." He glared at his son as though daring him to object to his interpretation.

And when his son remained silent, he leaned forward and said, "Now, this is important, and I want you to pay strict attention. You didn't know what was wrong with Moose when you saw him. After all, you're not a doctor. All you know is that he was lying there still. So your idea was to get out of there fast and get some help, call the police or a doctor. The idea that he might have been murdered never entered your head. All you know is that he didn't look right —"

"But it had to be murder, because somebody put that sheet over his head."

"You didn't see how they wrapped him in the first place, did you?"

"No, but —"

"Look, what I'm trying to tell you is that you were not involved with any of this. You didn't pick the place; you didn't break into the house; you went back to get Moose only because he was sick and you had a car; and finally when you saw he was very sick, your one thought was to get help for him."

"But Didi and Bill said —"

"You wouldn't be likely to remember what they said. All you remember was there was some talk about Moose and how they put him to bed. The details, you just don't remember. You weren't there; you didn't see anything; you don't know anything."

"Yeah, I just pussyfoot."

"That's it," said his father eagerly.

Stu rose. "And afterward, when it's all over, what do I do? Get myself a new set of friends or move to another town? And what do I do about living with myself? I'm just a dumb kid, and you're a smart big-time executive. Well, maybe you're too smart. Nobody, certainly not Lanigan, is going to believe that all I had were noble thoughts. If I'm not involved, then I'm damn sure Lanigan's not going to get me involved. Besides, I don't think you're worried about me, anyway." He went to the door, and from the threshold he said, "It's you, your reputation, you're worried about."

Mrs. Gorfinkle came in. "Oh —

348

where's Stu? Have you finished with him?''

''Yes, I've finished with him,'' her husband said between clenched teeth.

''What's the matter? Did you quarrel again?''

''You work and sweat and slave'' — but Gorfinkle was talking to himself — ''for what if not for your children? And what thanks do you get? To them you're a hypocrite. You're just thinking of yourself.''

# 49

Jenkins looked curiously from the rabbi to Lanigan. "Here's this guy been dumping on me all evening, and you wonder why I don't want to help get him home so his daddy won't know he'd been drinking? The way I felt it would have been better than a hootnanny to see his old man skin him alive. I don't believe this turn the other cheek business you religious types go in for, Rabbi."

"Neither do we. That's Christian doctrine. We regard it as condoning sin."

"Oh yeah?" He nodded. "That's interesting."

"You preferred to get back at him?" Lanigan suggested.

The Negro shrugged his shoulders. "I didn't give it no thought if you want to know. I just wanted to split. These were

350

kids — most of them nice kids — but kids.''

"You only wanted to get home," the rabbi offered.

"That's right. It'd been a pretty dreary evening. It wasn't the kids' fault, but on the other hand, they didn't help any. I just wanted out. So I picked up my bike at Didi's and took off. Well, I hadn't gone far when it started to rain. I could've gone back to Didi's, I suppose, but then I thought of that Hillson House, and I knew the door was open.''

"Which was nearer, Hillson House or Didi's?" asked the rabbi.

Jenkins shrugged. "What difference? Hillson House was on the way. Didi's meant going back.''

"And you weren't thinking about Moose lying there all nicely tied up and helpless?" asked Lanigan sarcastically.

"Not until after I got in," said Jenkins cheerfully.

"Yet you were careful to wheel your bike across the sidewalk and hide it behind the bushes.''

"Why sure, man, I had no right to be

in there for all the door was open." He looked from one to the other to see if they understood. "So I went in and put the latch on the door."

"Why did you do that?"

"They said the police come by and sometimes try the door. Then I looked out, and I see this car coming along. When he gets near the house, he slows down and just crawls by like he's trying to look in, maybe. But he rides on."

"Paff," said Lanigan in an aside to the rabbi. The rabbi nodded.

"That kind of frightened me," Jenkins went on, "so I pulled the shades down. I had a flashlight with me, but then I noticed I could still see some of the light from the streetlamp through the shades, so maybe somebody outside could see in. So I unhooked these heavy lined velvet drapes until it was pitch dark, and then I figured I was safe to use my flash."

"Did you go in the little room to see Moose? Was he all right?"

"I didn't have to see him; I could hear him snoring away. I peeked through the drapes, and this time I see this car parked right under the streetlamp, with a guy sitting at the wheel like he's got nothing but time."

"The same car?" asked Lanigan.

Jenkins shook his head. "I don't know. I just got a glimpse of the car the first time — mostly his headlights, but at the time I don't think it was the same one, because I started worrying about the third car."

"The third car?"

"Sure. I see one car, and he passes slow. I see another, and he stops and waits. You know the drill. Trouble comes in threes. And the third car that comes along, the guy is bound to come in." He looked at his questioners, satisfied that his logic was unassailable and that they would understand.

"And all this time you never once thought about Moose?" Lanigan's voice showed disbelief.

"Sure, I thought about him," said Jenkins. "I thought about him lying there, as you say, nice and helpless."

"Ah." Lanigan hitched his chair forward.

"I thought I ought to get some of my own back. Some stupid kid trick, but just something to make me feel better. If I'd had my paints with me, I would have painted his face black, maybe. That cracked me up — the thought of seeing his look when the kids found him like that. I thought of giving him a haircut maybe, something special, like trimming my initials in that whiffle of his, or maybe just pinching his shoes and hiding them on him. But, of course, that would have meant unwrapping him, and I didn't want to do that."

"Naturally," said Lanigan drily.

"You think I was afraid of him?"

"The thought had crossed my mind," said Lanigan.

Jenkins shook his head. "I wouldn't fight him fair and square. Why should I? He had fifty pounds on me. But if we'd been alone together down the beach and he'd started to crack wise, I would have gone after him with a rock. I couldn't with the kids there. They'd have stopped it."

"But they weren't there now."

"That's right. And I started to get mad.

There I had this wonderful chance, and there was nothing I could do. So then I remembered about his cigarette case, and I decided to take it so it shouldn't be a total loss."

"You took his cigarette case?"

"Yeah, I'd noticed it earlier in the evening. One side had cigarettes and one side had sticks."

"Sticks?" asked the rabbi.

"That's right, pot."

"He was smoking those during the evening?" asked Lanigan.

"Oh no, he smoked the regulars, but I'd spotted the others. I was going down to New York the next morning, and I figured they'd come in handy. The case was in his shirt pocket, and I just slid it out. And when I came back in the living room and peeked through the curtains again, I see the car is gone. Believe me, I didn't wait. I lit right out of there."

"You unlatched the door for Gorfinkle and Jacobs, of course," suggested the rabbi.

Jenkins smiled and shook his head. "What would I do that for? No, I left it locked. They were just coming to rescue this Moose. Why make it easy for them?''

# 50

The young man was indignant. "I see him bring the prisoner in, and I try to get a pic, and this Lieutenant Jennings blocks me. Then I ask the chief for a statement, and he says, 'No statement now.' So I figure I'll hang around and speak to him when things quiet down a little. So then — now get this: A guy that one of the cops tells me is the rabbi of the local synagogue comes in and goes into Lanigan's office. And pretty soon Lanigan and this rabbi come out, and the two of them go down to the cellblock to question the prisoner. I try to go along, and Lanigan shuts the door in my face. If a rabbi can be present while the prisoner is being questioned — and he's not Jewish, because he's colored, so he can't be his spiritual adviser, that's for sure — why can't a reporter?"

"All right. Let it go." Harvey Kanter dismissed the young man and reached for the telephone. "Hello, Hugh? Harvey Kanter. How are you?"

"Okay, and you?"

"Never better. And the missus?"

"She's fine."

"What do you hear from the boy?"

"Turning the West Coast upside down according to his last letter."

"Good. Hey, what are you doing Sunday night?"

"Nothing that I know of."

"Well, Edith is planning a regular seafood dinner — clam chowder, steamers, lobsters — the works. How about you and the missus coming over?"

"Sounds good, but isn't it your holiday?"

"Come to think of it." He chuckled. "I got a brother-in-law who's president of a synagogue, and I got to call a Catholic to tell me it's the seder. But I haven't kept it for so long I wouldn't know how to start. I'll scrounge around and find a skullcap for you if it'll make you feel any better. Is it a date?"

"Oh, sure, but I'll have to check with Gladys —"

"Edith will call her. Say, while I've got you on the line, what is this I hear you been doing to my boy? He tells me you won't give him the right time."

"He's pushy, Harvey. Why don't you teach him some manners down there?"

Kanter chuckled. "We don't teach them anything these days. They come from a school of journalism, and they know it all. He's a good kid, but he's been watching *The Front Page* on the late-night movie, and he thinks he's Hildy Johnson. He tells me you've got Jenkins. Did he talk?"

"Oh, he talked, all right . . ."

Kanter reached for a pencil and a pad of paper.

# 51

"He's lying. I just don't buy the idea of him going out to Hillson House to get in out of the rain and then sitting around in the living room doing nothing except peer out into the street every now and then to see if the car has gone, entirely content with having scored on Moose because he's pinched his cigarette case. If that's all he was planning to do, why all this business of latching the door —?"

"The police might —"

"All right, I'll let that go, but why pull down the shades and then draw the drapes? No, Rabbi, I've got a different idea of how he spent those twenty minutes. It's my feeling that he came in there the way he says, all right, but he took all these elaborate precautions with the drapes and all because he was planning to be there for some time. He went into the room where Moose was, pinched his cigarette case, and then put that plastic sheet over his head — as he'd been thinking all along — and then came back to the living room to wait.''

''For whom?''

''Not for whom, Rabbi, for what. He came back to wait until Moose stopped breathing. Motive, opportunity, method — he had them all. And what's more, that remark he made to Jacobs about covering his head when they swaddled him up in the first place — that's going to prove premeditation. I put it to you, isn't it damn funny that this Jenkins, who wouldn't have anything to do with helping Moose get home, was ready to help put him to bed there at Hillson House? Why didn't he say then, 'To hell with him. Let him lie on the floor'? We didn't inquire into it, but I'll bet when we start preparing this case, we'll find it was Jenkins who suggested swaddling him up in the first place.''

''Yes, I suppose you will,'' said the rabbi sadly. ''I'm sure that, without

361

meaning to be unfair and with no thought that you're in fact being unfair, you'll suggest it to Jacobs, and he'll come to believe that it's true."

"You're saying that it's easy to believe what you'd like to believe. All right," said Lanigan. "I'll admit it's possible. It's a normal human failing. But it cuts both ways. It's just as wrong to refuse to see evidence because it points to someone you feel sorry for. In any case, it's a minor point. You haven't shown me what's wrong with my reasoning."

"What's wrong? The boys, Gorfinkle and Jacobs, found the door unlatched and ajar. Jenkins said he set the latch so it would lock. He wouldn't lie about something like that. It would be pointless."

"Sometimes the lock doesn't catch. The wind could have blown it open."

"All right. The boys said they found the body with the head covered. That's how they knew it was murder. If Jenkins did it and waited to make sure Moose was dead, why didn't he then remove that part of the sheet once the boy had smothered? That would be the obvious thing to do. Then it would have looked like an accidental death. To leave it over his head was to leave proof that it was murder. He's a bright lad; he'd realize he would be likely to get involved."

Lanigan shrugged his shoulders. "He might have panicked."

"After he calmly sat around for twenty minutes or so?"

"How do you know it was calmly? He may have been in a panic all along. How do we know he did stay there for twenty minutes? Moose would have used up the available oxygen in that plastic sheet in a lot less time than that. And this car that he said he saw parked in front of the house — I don't believe it. What would anyone be doing there at that time of night and on such a night? If it were a couple who stopped to do a little necking, they wouldn't have parked underneath the streetlamp. I think he put that in to suggest to us that someone entered Hillson House after he left."

Lanigan shook his head. "No, Rabbi, stick to the essentials. He was sore because

Moose — what's the term the kids use? Dumped, that's it — dumped on him. The idea of covering his head was in his mind, because he made the remark. Remember, he didn't deny making it. He wanted to get even with Moose. He admits that. He even admits going into the room where Moose was lying. And while he was looking down on him, he thought of the things Moose had said, and he picked up that last fold of the sheet and pulled it over his head and tucked it in. And if you don't think it happened that way, you've got to come up with some mysterious stranger who somehow knows that Moose is there, who can get into the house, who knows that Moose is conveniently tied up and then covers his head." He paused an impressive moment. "The only ones who fit that set of particulars, Rabbi, are your two young friends, Gorfinkle and Jacobs."

# 52

They were not hostile to the idea; they were just not enthusiastic. And it bothered Roger Epstein. "I don't understand," he said, "we're supposed to be all for social action." He turned to Brennerman. "You said that you wanted to see the temple involved. And you, Ben, social action is supposed to be the key to your whole program. Are you interested only when it's at a distance, someplace down South?"

"No, of course not, Roger," said Gorfinkle easily. "It's just that the key word is justice. Now you heard the news broadcast; what's more, I called my brother-in-law to check on that report, and he said it was accurate. He got it himself from Lanigan. Now, maybe I'm wrong, but my impression is that this colored fellow — what's his name? Jenkins — my impression is that Jenkins is guilty as all hell. You get a bunch of red-necks down in some Southern town framing some boy because he's colored, and I'm prepared to go all out. But this fellow was caught dead to rights."

"That's the way I feel," said Brennerman.

"Me too," said Jacobs.

"I don't see how you can be so sure," Epstein began.

"Aw, come," said Gorfinkle. "You don't believe, you don't really believe, that he'd go back there just to steal a handful of cigarettes, do you?"

"And remember," Jacobs pointed out, "our own kids are involved in this, Roger — your Didi as well as my Bill and Ben's boy, Stu."

"Sure, and what if one of them found himself in the position of this boy?" demanded Epstein. "I don't care whether he did it or not; he still has the right to a fair trial."

"He'll get one, won't he? This is Massachusetts. There won't be any funny stuff here, no lynch mob —"

"What kind of a fair trial can he get when he doesn't even have a lawyer?" demanded Epstein.

"If that's what's worrying you, forget it," said Gorfinkle. "As far as I know, he hasn't been formally charged yet. When he is, the court will appoint a lawyer if he doesn't have one or if he can't afford one."

"Sure, I understand there's a fixed fee for that kind of legal service, something like five hundred dollars. And you know what kind of lawyer he'll get — some kid just out of law school who maybe hasn't tried a case yet."

"What do you want us to do, Roger?"

"I want us to show that we mean what we say and have the courage of our convictions. Jenkins has the right to a good lawyer, a good trial lawyer, someone like Warren Donohue, say. I'd like for us to start a Jenkins Defense Committee to raise funds so we could get him. You mark my words, before this is over a lot of the more liberal churches are going to get involved in this. So why can't we be the first, instead of tagging along after the others?"

Gorfinkle pursed his lips and considered. "Well, you know, you might just have something there. But Donohue's fee comes high."

"So what?" Brennerman was excited now.

"And can we get him?"

"If we can raise his fee," said Jacobs, "why not? Our money's as good as the next guy's."

"And if we set up a Defense Committee, we can raise his fee," said Brennerman, "if we go about it right."

"We could solicit funds from the entire community," said Epstein, "but it would have to be a temple project, not just something we as individuals are sponsoring."

"And that ties right into our program!" exclaimed Brennerman.

"Now that presents problems," said Gorfinkle, "because if we offer it as a temple project, the rabbi is going to have something to say about it. And right now, my stock isn't exactly soaring with our rabbi. As a matter of fact, so far as he knows he's on his way out at the next board meeting."

"Yeah, I'm afraid you jumped the gun, Ben," said Brennerman gloomily. "You shouldn't have fired him —"

"I didn't fire him," said Gorfinkle, "I just warned him. And if this whole business hadn't come up, I still think it was the right thing to do."

"We all agreed to it, remember," said Jacobs, "so don't go blaming Ben."

"Well, mind you, I'm not blaming you, Ben," said Epstein, "but I'm inclined to think that regardless of the present situation, we acted too fast. I for one feel funny about it."

To Gorfinkle this was criticism from an unexpected source. "What is it you feel funny about, Roger?" he asked quietly.

"I feel funny about the whole deal. I feel funny about me, a new man at this temple business, firing the rabbi, who's been involved with it all his life. I feel funny about being chairman of the Ritual Committee. In a way, that's what set the whole business off, but I certainly never thought it would split the congregation. If I had, I wouldn't have let you talk me into it. Well, maybe it's not too late to repair the damage. I'm bowing out as of right now."

"Bowing out of what?" demanded Jacobs.

"I'm declining the nomination for chairman of the Ritual Committee. And I'm not waiting for you to announce it at the next board meeting. I think, considering what the nomination resulted in, I ought to tell the rabbi myself. It would be a good chance to get him behind this Defense Committee, and maybe he'll figure a way to speak to Paff and his group and pull the pieces together."

"You mean you think I ought to keep Paff as chairman? Is that your idea, Roger?" asked Gorfinkle.

"No, but I don't see why you can't get someone else, someone who's neutral. How about Wasserman?"

"Yeah, how about Wasserman?" said Brennerman.

"Well . . ."

# 53

They were playing halfheartedly, their minds not on the game. Quite early in the evening Irving Kallen pushed his chair back. "I've had enough," he said. "I just can't seem to get interested."

"Once around?" asked Paff.

"If you want."

Dr. Edelstein pushed back from the table, too. "What's the point, Meyer? Personally, I'd rather have a cup of coffee."

"That's easy enough," said Paff. He tilted back in his chair and called out to his wife in another room, "How about some coffee for the boys, Laura?" He gathered in the cards that were lying on the table and riffled them. "I was in Chelsea yesterday, and I bumped into this fellow I know — his brother is a rabbi, a real Orthodox type — and I happened to mention about somebody dying in a place that was going to be used for a synagogue. According to him, he didn't think that ruled it out. He said he'd ask his brother, though."

"Forget it, Meyer," said Kermit Arons. "Hillson House is out. Remember, it wasn't just somebody dying. After all, in our own temple, you remember Arthur Barron had a heart attack — was it two years ago?"

"Three years ago," said Doc Edelstein. "But he didn't die in the sanctuary. We took him to the hospital, and I pronounced him dead there."

"It doesn't make any difference. The point is that he just died. Here, you had a murder. It wouldn't make any difference if the entire Board of Rabbis pronounced it okay. For years to come that house will be known as the place where somebody was murdered. Who'll you get to join that kind of a temple? To tell the truth, I'd feel funny myself, wondering if my seat was where the kid got it."

"So where does it leave us?" asked Paff.

"I guess right back where we started from," said Kallen. He brightened. "You know, you didn't plan it that way, Meyer, I mean that we should sit tight at the last meeting, but when you come right down to it, it was a smart move. If we had actually kicked up a fuss when Gorfinkle announced the new committees, we'd have to eat crow now."

"I don't see that there's any real problem," Edelstein offered. "Irv is right. We're right back where we started from. We never made any official announcement about any new temple; we didn't walk out when the new committees were announced. We sat tight, and we can continue to sit tight."

"That's right."

"What the hell —"

"You want I should sit by and let those guys do just as they please?" demanded Paff.

"We'll still be able to oppose them on the board," said Edelstein.

"Yeah, fat lot of good that will do us where they've got a clear majority."

"You mean they're going to go ahead

with calling for the rabbi's resignation at the next meeting?'' asked Edelstein. ''Frankly, I think that's pretty rotten after all the work he did for the kids, and —''

''What work?'' asked Arons. ''He got young Gorfinkle and young Jacobs to give their story to the cops. I personally think it was the right thing to do, but a lot of the parents of the other kids were pretty sore about it. I certainly don't think Gorfinkle or Jacobs were too pleased. Fortunately, they got this colored guy, but if it hadn't been for that —''

''Then you think they will go ahead with the resignation?'' asked Edelstein.

''No-o,'' said Arons. ''I'm inclined to think they'll let it rest for the time being. You see, where the case isn't settled yet and the rabbi is such good friends with the police chief, it would be kind of foolish to let him go. My guess is that they'll just wait until his contract runs out and then won't renew.''

''By God, we'll make them renew!'' said Paff.

''Since when are you so keen on the rabbi?'' asked Arons.

"I'm not," snapped Paff. "Never was and never will be. But you're missing the point."

"What point? They're going to drop him."

"They're going to try to drop him, you mean," Paff amended.

"But they got a clear majority on the board."

"Yes," said Paff, "and there we can't beat them. But the question of dropping a rabbi who has served the congregation for six years already, who has the respect of the Gentile community — that doesn't have to be kept a strictly board matter. That's something that the whole membership is interested in. Now, I don't know how popular the rabbi is, but I know it's a lot harder to fire somebody than it is to let him stay on. Nobody likes to fire."

"So?"

"So that gives us an issue that we got a chance to win on. And if we win and the rabbi remains, we've evened up the odds, because when we oppose them, they just outvote us, but when he opposes them, he usually makes it a matter of ritual law or Jewish principle, and he sticks to it until they knuckle under."

Edelstein smiled. Kallen considered the proposition and then nodded his agreement. Arons said, "It's an idea, Meyer; it's an idea."

# 54

All week long the Small household had been busy with the cleaning and scrubbing and lining of shelves and cupboards that were normal preparation for the Passover week. The rabbi helped as much as possible, bringing up the rickety ladder from the basement and handing down to Miriam the stacks of Passover dishes and utensils that were kept on the topmost shelf of the cupboard for use only during the Passover week. The brunt of the work naturally fell on Miriam, and this year it was even more difficult, because Jonathan was old enough to follow her around and get in the way and continually demand attention. But finally, Saturday night, they had finished. While Miriam luxuriated on the living room couch the rabbi, followed step by step by his young son, had gone about the ritual symbolic search for the *chometz,* the crumbs of leaven left lying around on purpose to be found by candlelight, and with a feather swept onto a wooden spoon, which would be burned the next morning.

"Do you want me to take Jonathan off your hands, David?" Miriam called to him, with no real thought her offer would be accepted.

"Oh no, I always helped my father search for the *chometz* when I was a youngster. Kids like it. Do you remember where I put the candle and the — never mind, I've got them." He recited the benediction. "Blessed art Thou, O Lord . . . Who commanded us to remove the leaven," and then as his small son watched wide-eyed, by the flickering light of his candle he swept the leaven from the shelf where it had been previously placed and wrapped it in a bit of cloth and put it aside. He recited the ancient formula: "All manner of leaven that is in my possession which I have not seen or removed shall be null and accounted as the dust of the earth."

"Tomorrow," he said to Jonathan, "you can watch us burn it." And he called to his wife and asked her to get him ready for bed. Mr. Epstein was due any moment.

The rabbi shook his head. "I'm sorry, Mr. Epstein. I know you mean well, but I think you're making a serious mistake —"

"I don't understand, Rabbi. We've got to help Alan Jenkins the best way we can. We're involved. My Didi invited him, and all the kids there were our kids."

"Then why don't you force the jail?"

"That's ridiculous, Rabbi."

"Precisely. And yet that would really help him. What I'm saying is that not all well-meaning actions necessarily result in the greatest good. You tell me that you have engaged this Donohue to act for him. I've heard of him; who hasn't? And now you tell me he's going to demand a change of venue on the grounds that the young man can't get a fair trial in this community? Well, I don't want the Jewish community to go on record as doubting the good faith of the town. We have been here for some years now, and there has never been anything to suggest that. But I'll tell you what your action does suggest. It suggests that you're pretty sure that Jenkins is guilty. If he is, he should be convicted, but until all the evidence is in, I for one intend to keep an open mind."

"But this change of venue — that's just a standard tactic."

"Yes, but what you consider a standard tactic someone else might regard as an unfair tactic. That's what's wrong with your whole social action concept, if I may say so. You're not satisfied with doing what you can; you must have everyone else in the temple doing it, too. Our religion has an ethical code, a guideline for conduct, Mr. Epstein, but it is the individual who implements it according to the dictates of his conscience and his own intelligence. One person may join a picket line and another no less interested in the same cause may feel better results are to be gained through the courts or private negotiations or by making contributions. It is a matter for the individual to decide. Even in our services we pray as individuals rather than in a chorus. You can mount a campaign and make a plea for funds, but so long as a single member of the congregation opposes, you have no right to make it in the name of the temple, regardless of how big a majority you can muster on the board of directors."

"I don't understand you, David." Miriam pressed her fist against her mouth, as though to stifle harsh words of reproof. "He came to make amends. He was trying so hard to effect a reconciliation. And he's a good man."

"Of course, he's a good man. And so are Gorfinkle and the rest of them. They're all good men, or they wouldn't be so concerned about what may happen to a poor Negro that stumbled into a mess of trouble. But goodness is not enough. The people who took part in the religious wars were good men, but they killed and maimed in the tens of thousands nevertheless."

"Oh, David, you're so — so inflexible. Can't you bend a little?"

He looked at her in surprise. "I bend

when I have to, and I can. But I've got to be careful not to bend so far that I'll fall over.''

# 55

On Sundays the minyan was held at nine instead of seven thirty, as it was on weekday mornings. Although it was a lovely day and he had plenty of time to walk, the rabbi took his car. He did not go directly to the temple, but drove along the shore, stopping once or twice along the way to enjoy the sight of the waves breaking against the rocks and the gulls swooping down low over the water.

The road hugged the shore and then fell away, and he looked ahead and realized that he was approaching Hillson House. He slowed down as he came abreast of it and for a moment thought of stopping to look around. But he saw a man standing at the window of the adjoining house, talking into a telephone, so he drove on.

He arrived just in time for the service. Sundays always drew a larger crowd, because many fathers who brought their children to the Sunday school attended the minyan for lack of anything better to do while waiting to take them home. Today the short service was followed by a collation, given by one of the regular members in honor of his daughter's engagement.

They stood around, sipping their tea or coffee, munching cake and cookies, unleavened, of course, in keeping with the Passover regulation, since the holiday began that evening. Arthur Nussbaum was there, still pushing his pet project. "Look, fellows, I tell you it makes no sense to keep all that dough just sitting in a bank —"

"It's earning interest, isn't it?"

"So every year costs go up twice as much. Sooner or later, everybody knows we're going to change those seats. If we had gone ahead when the money was first left to us, we could have done half the sanctuary, right up to the center aisle. This year the money probably wouldn't cover more than a third."

"Yeah, fat chance of having some seats of one kind and the rest another. It will look terrible. The women will raise Cain."

"Let 'em. Don't you see," Nussbaum urged, "if they think it looks funny, they'll work all the harder to get the rest put in."

"Yeah? Well, if you think there was a stink about permanent seating, just wait till the first third of the sanctuary is fancied up with one kind of seat —"

The rabbi, who was standing nearby, murmured, "So why does it have to be the first third? Why not start replacing the seats from the rear?" He spotted Paff leaving the chapel and excused himself.

Nussbaum overheard the remark and repeated it to the others.

"Is he kidding?"

"That would be even worse. That would guarantee getting everyone sore."

"Not as sore as our present seats," said Dr. Edelstein. "You put padded seats in back, and you can put me down for one right now."

Irving Kallen nodded. "You may have

something at that, Doc. For me I don't care. I'm well-padded, but my old man, I'd bet he'd really appreciate it."

"When you come down to it," said Nussbaum slowly, "it's only fair."

Brennerman, who was standing by, pursed his lips, then suddenly broke into a delighted roar of laughter. "By God, Nussbaum, you're right. The rabbi's come up with the perfect solution!"

They all looked at him.

"Don't you see it, boys? Front row *yicchus,* back row *tuchus.* Suit yourself!" Laughing loudly, he spotted Gorfinkle and hurried over to tell him what had happened.

The rabbi hailed Paff and led him to a side corridor. When they were a safe distance from the others, he said, "I read your statement to the police, Mr. Paff. Judging from the names of those people you listed as partners in your business deal, I suspect you were interested in Hillson House as a possible new temple."

Paff grinned. "That's right, Rabbi, but of course, it's out of the question now.

We're letting the whole matter drop for the time being." He thought of something. "I was going to tell you, of course, but Becker reported that you weren't interested anyway."

"That's all right," the rabbi hastened to assure him. "I wasn't, and I'm not. My reason for questioning you is that I wanted to clarify some things in my own mind with respect to this case. You told the police that you slowed down as you approached Hillson House and then drove on. Is that correct?"

"Yes?"

"You didn't stop?"

Paff considered. "I may have stopped for a moment."

"You're quite sure you didn't stop for much longer than a moment?"

"What are you getting at, Rabbi?"

"I'm suggesting that you stopped for quite a while, perhaps fifteen or twenty minutes or even longer."

"Why do you say that?"

"Because as it stands your statement doesn't ring true. I passed Hillson House on my way over to the temple this morning. That's a straight stretch of road, no turn, nothing blocking your vision. Even in a rainstorm, long before you reached Hillson House by whichever direction you approached, you could see whether someone was waiting there or not. So there was no need for you to slow down. And since you expected to meet someone there, I suggest that you would have waited for fifteen minutes anyway."

"All right, suppose I did?"

"Then the police might wonder why you didn't bother to go inside in all that time."

"I didn't. I swear I didn't, Rabbi."

"Why not?"

His face showed resignation. "I don't really know. I've been by there any number of times, but I guess it was during the daytime, and it always looked bright and cheerful. And this night it was all dark, and it was raining, and I just didn't like the idea of going in alone."

"Then why didn't you tell the police the truth?"

"You know how it is, Rabbi. I heard that Moose had been found in there. Well, he worked for me, and I knew him. If I said I had been waiting around there for half an hour or so, they'd begin to ask me questions: Did I hear anything? Did I see anything? Why didn't I go in? No, I just didn't want to get involved."

"Well, I'd say you were involved now. If I were you, I'd go down to the police and tell them you'd like to change your statement."

"But that would mean that I was lying, and that would look suspicious."

"It will look a lot more suspicious when they find out the truth."

Paff sighed. "I suppose you're right, Rabbi."

# 56

When he arrived home, he found Lanigan waiting for him.

"I thought those morning prayer services of yours only last about half an hour," the chief of police complained.

"There was a collation afterward," said the rabbi, "and then I had to perform an errand of mercy; I went to visit the sick. Sorry you had to wait. Is it business or purely social?"

Lanigan grinned. "I guess it's always a little bit of both when I come visiting. I understand, Rabbi, that there's a movement afoot to set up a Jenkins Defense Committee. You know anything about it?"

"Yes, as a matter of fact, I do. Why, do you object to it?"

"Well, of course, every man has a right

— yes, I object to it!" said Lanigan. "I know this Donohue. He'll stir up a lot of trouble and maybe create an atmosphere in this town that we might be years getting over. And none of it will do Jenkins any good. It will just be a lot of propaganda about social justice and the rights of the underprivileged and Lord knows what all. And it won't have any bearing on this case, because Jenkins is going to get a fair trial, and it's got nothing to do with whether he's black, white, or green with yellow polka dots."

"I'm not sure. Are you giving him a fair shake? It seems to me that you've made up your mind that he's guilty —"

"I don't decide whether he's guilty or not. That's up to a judge and jury. But naturally I have an opinion. I've dealt fairly with him throughout. You were present when I questioned him. Did I browbeat him? I practically begged him to get a lawyer. He didn't want one."

"But when he told his story, didn't you automatically assume those parts that indicated he was guilty were true and those that suggested he might be innocent a pack of lies?"

"You've always got to choose from the available material what you'll believe and what you won't. You know that. Take Jenkins' statement that there was somebody parked right across the street for about twenty minutes —"

"That's true."

"How do you mean?"

The rabbi told of his conversation with Paff.

Lanigan strode around the room as he thought aloud. "That means Paff might have seen Jenkins enter the house and waited there to see what would happen. When Jenkins doesn't come out, he rides off? So that leaves him on the scene with transportation to return and no real alibi —" He shook his head vigorously. "No, I don't believe it, Rabbi. You wouldn't throw a member of your congregation to the wolves just like that. You must have something else in mind."

"I'm merely suggesting that there are other possibilities. You yourself suggested Gorfinkle and Jacobs. The point is that Jenkins is not the only one whose actions are suspect; besides, your case against him is full of holes."

"Like what?"

"How about the death of that man in Boston? How does Jenkins fit into that?"

"I don't say he had anything to do with that. His death and the connection with Moose — that's pure coincidence."

"Coincidences happen, but not often. But the big objection to your case against Jenkins is that the next door neighbor, this —"

"Mr. Begg?"

"Yes, Mr. Begg. He saw a light. That's what led him to call the police."

Lanigan looked puzzled for a moment, and then his face cleared. "Oh, I see what you're getting at — that someone came to the house after Jenkins left, that *he* put on the light, and that *he* presumably killed Moose — maybe your Mr. Paff. It's a good effort, Rabbi, but here's where I demolish it. Jenkins said that he drew the shades and the drapes before he put on a light. Right?"

"Right."

"And there was no reason for him to lie

about something like that."

"Agreed."

"So if someone, Paff or a mysterious stranger, had put on a light, it would not have shown."

"Precisely. Then how could Begg have seen a light?"

"Huh?"

"The youngsters were all agreed that they did not put on a light. Jenkins used a flashlight but only after he had drawn the drapes —"

"Then how could Begg have seen a light in the house?"

"That was my question," said the rabbi pointedly. "But I can suggest an answer. The only way he could have seen a light with all the windows blocked off was by having himself been in the house and put them on."

"You saying —"

"I'm saying that he entered the house after Jenkins left. Since as the caretaker he must have had a key, the locked door presented no problem. He snapped on the light on entering and then went through each of the rooms. I'm suggesting that he put the plastic sheet over the boy's head, and then, leaving the lights on as an excuse to call the police, he hurried back to his own house, where there was a phone."

"And forgot to close the front door?"

"No, left it ajar purposely, I imagine, either on the chance of the cruising car spotting it — in which case, he would not be involved even as informer — or perhaps so as not to raise any immediate question of how the murderer had got in."

Lanigan massaged his square chin with a big red hand as he checked back over the rabbi's reasoning. Then he grinned. "You had me going there for a minute, Rabbi. It all sounds plausible except" — he held up an admonishing forefinger — "that he called from his own house. On the way back, he would have noticed that there was no light coming through the windows of Hillson House, because the blinds were drawn."

The rabbi nodded. "Yes, and the phone is in a room which overlooks Hillson House. I drove by this morning and saw him at the window, phone in hand. So standing there, talking to the police, he'd certainly notice that there was no light coming from the windows of Hillson House. And the explanation is that there is where a real coincidence occurred."

"What coincidence?"

"That while he was still inside Hillson House, or just as he left, all the lights in that part of town went out."

"You mean the transformer blowing?"

"M-hm. That was the only coincidence."

"How about his happening to go over there?"

"That was no coincidence. He went right after Jenkins left *because* Jenkins left. I mean he may have seen Jenkins leave or heard him starting up his motorcycle, right next door so to speak, so he hurried over to investigate. It looked all right; the door was locked and it was dark. But, of course, he had to make sure. He had a key and went in. Naturally, he put on the lights. Maybe he listened for a moment or called out. Then he went for a look around and found Moose. Since he wanted the body found immediately, that very night —"

"Why did it have to be that night?"

"Because if he waited a day or two, he himself would have to find the body — he was the caretaker. This way, it would be the police who would find the body, and if they came that night, they would see fresh evidence of someone having been there — cigarette butts, beer cans."

Lanigan smiled. "Nice work, Rabbi. I'll add Begg to my list of Jenkins, Paff, Carter, and seven assorted kids. While chewing the fat with Eban Jennings, my lieutenant, I made as good a case against each of those others. But, of course, they all have flaws. For instance, Begg couldn't have known that Moose was in Hillson House, now could he?"

The rabbi shook his head.

"So if he had some reason for killing Moose, which you haven't bothered to mention, by the way, how would he have known to go in there? The normal thing, if he thought someone had broken into the place, was to call the police and ask them to check."

"I suppose because he had to go there.

Before calling the police, he had to make sure that nothing had been taken.''

"Like what?"

"Like marihuana. He'd be more likely to cache it there than keep it in his own house."

"But Mr. Begg? A pusher? Oh, that's impossible, Rabbi." His face showed utter incredulity. "He's an old-time resident of the town, a crusty Yankee."

The rabbi's grin was derisive. "And former teacher and former selectman who couldn't do anything wrong. It must be an outsider, a stranger."

"All right, I suppose I deserve that," said Lanigan, "but what I really meant is that — that he's a cantankerous sort of man who's always in our hair. If he were engaged in something like pot peddling, he wouldn't be calling attention to himself."

The rabbi shrugged off the argument. "Protective coloration. It evidently worked better than to try to be unobtrusive, especially in a small town like this. He always had the reputation of being a crank, so he went on being one when he began selling this stuff. It was safer than suddenly changing his image."

Lanigan was silent, then he said quietly, "What made you think of him? Did you work this out by this Talmudic pil — whatever it is?"

"Pilpul? Not at all. I thought of Begg because he was the most obvious suspect. You would have seen it, too, if you weren't conditioned to focus first and foremost on the outsider, the stranger, Alan Jenkins, who was not only from outside the town, but also colored."

"But Begg is a kind of outsider. He's a kind of recluse and a nut."

"Not at all. He's eccentric but well within the acceptable. He's even traditional — the hard-headed, cantankerous Yankee who sticks up for his rights."

"But what did he do that made you suspect him?"

"For one thing, he runs a place where youngsters hang out. He sells soda and some school supplies and lets them play the pinball machines. You've seen the place. What is there in that that makes it possible for him to even pay the rent? For another, Moose came from his house. He had to, because the tide was in and he couldn't have come from farther along the beach. And then when the youngsters were breaking into the house and they were worried that they might be seen by someone next door, remember it was Moose who assured them that Begg wouldn't bother them. Begg, a known crank and buttinsky. How could he possibly know that? Only if he knew Begg was going to leave. They probably left at the same time. And finally, I began thinking of Begg because it seemed odd that he should call to report he had seen a light. Unless he were a timid man, I would have assumed that he would first have investigated himself or at least reconnoitered.''

''Then, according to you, there's a cache of marihuana in Hillson House.''

The rabbi shook his head. ''There was. I assume he removed it before calling the police. That's why he had to go there. and by this time, he wouldn't have it in his own house either.''

''You realize, of course,'' said Lanigan,

"that there isn't a particle of evidence against him. If we find his fingerprints in Hillson House, he says he's been there many times as caretaker."

"You might ask him about seeing the light."

Once again Lanigan got up to stride around the room. "That's not evidence. He has only to insist that he either saw it or thought he saw it. No jury would convict a man for saying he saw a light that he couldn't have seen. They'd assume a natural mistake, the headlight of a car, the reflection of a streetlamp. No, it's a pity we can't introduce this pilpul of yours as legal evidence."

"We could try."

Lanigan hitched his chair up and said eagerly, "For instance?"

"Well, this man in Boston who was murdered the same day. We might think about him for a while to good effect."

"Wilcox?"

"Yes, Wilcox. We know Moose went to see him because of the two twenty-dollar bills."

"And the marihuana."

"Marihuana he could have got from any number of sources, but two twenty-dollar bills whose serial numbers ran consecutive with those Wilcox had — those could have come only from Wilcox."

"All right."

"How did Moose get them?" asked the rabbi.

"What do you mean?"

"He could have taken them, or they could have been given to him."

"Oh, I see. Well, obviously they were given to him, because if he had taken them, why stop at just two?"

"Precisely. Now why were they given to him? Two of them, mind you."

"We can't know that, Rabbi."

"Let me put it another way. Suppose in the course of conversation Moose had mentioned that he was broke. Conceivably, Wilcox might have been willing to lend him some to tide him over. Normally, that would mean a dollar or two, or five dollars, or even ten. But if he had nothing smaller on him at the time than twenties, he might have given him one of those. But he gave him two twenties — forty dollars. What does that suggest?''

Lanigan shook his head. ''I pass.''

''It suggests payment for something. But since Moose was broke and had nothing Wilcox could want, it suggests some sort of payment in advance.''

''For what?''

''We can't be certain, of course, but didn't you say this Wilcox was connected with the drug traffic?''

''The Boston police are sure he was a dealer.''

''All right, and since you also found a rather sizable quantity of the marihuana on Moose, and Jenkins admits having taken ten cigarettes from him, I suggest this was either an advance on salary or on commissions on sales. Mrs. Carter said that Moose had gone to Boston for a job. I think he got it.''

''Yeah, could be. Could be he was setting him up in business. All right, I'll buy that. What's the connection with his death? And with Begg?''

''We haven't finished with Moose's activities,'' said the rabbi reproachfully.

"Why, what did he do then?"

"He came back to Barnard's Crossing and went directly to see Mr. Begg."

"Any more on Moose?"

The rabbi shook his head. "I didn't know the young man. I can only speculate that the description of his behavior at the cookout, his drinking and carrying on there and again at the Hillson House, suggests he was euphoric. And when you add the fact he neglected to go home to dinner, which was a serious offense in the Carter household, it indicates he no longer had reason to fear his father."

"And Begg?" Lanigan asked sarcastically. "Do you know what he did? Where he went after he left Moose?"

"I'm afraid it would be pure speculation," said the rabbi primly.

"I see. Well, why stop now? Go ahead and speculate."

"Very well, I imagine he went to see Wilcox. The fact that Moose came to see Begg directly after leaving a narcotics dealer who had just set him up in business suggests that Begg was another agent of Wilcox, or a partner. If he were an agent, he certainly would have objected to anyone sharing the territory, Moose particularly. And if he were a partner, he may have gone to protest an injudicious appointment."

Lanigan sat back and stared at the rabbi in silence. Finally he said, "I don't suppose you'd care to amplify that with a fact or two, would you? Or did you mention something I happened to overlook?"

The rabbi grinned good-naturedly. "I said it was pure speculation, but if we consider it from the other end, it may seem more reasonable. For example, it gives us the first real motive for killing Moose. When Begg left his house, Moose knew where Begg was going, and when he heard of the death of Wilcox, he would know who did it."

Lanigan stared at the rabbi in silence. Finally he said, "So now you've got Begg killing Wilcox, too."

"It adds up."

"And proof?"

"Perhaps fingerprints, Begg's, in Wilcox's apartment?"

Lanigan shook his head. "Not after a week, with cops all over the place."

"Just a minute. Didn't you say some woman had seen him?"

"Madelaine Spinney. The Boston police thought they had something when she recognized Moose from a photograph they got from the files of the Boston papers. It's a different size than rogue's gallery pictures. That's probably why she picked it; it was different. From what they say, I doubt if she'd be able to identify your man. She's not very bright."

"Maybe he would identify her," suggested the rabbi.

## 57

"His car is in the driveway? . . . Good,
then he's home."

"Now, how do you want us to work it,
Chief?" asked the Boston detective.

"Just drive along, and when you come
to the house, stop," said Lanigan. "Keep
your motor running, just as you would if
you stopped to ask someone for
directions. Madelaine will get out. The
house will be on her side. Keep your coat
buttoned and push the collar up,
Madelaine. That's fine. Put your head
down a little. That's right. Then you just
go up and ring the bell. When the door
opens and he answers, you let him get a
good look at you and ask how to get onto
the road to Boston. Nothing to be afraid
of. The worst he can do is slam the door
in your face." He turned to the

policeman. "You just sit tight unless you see something unusual."

"Like what?"

"Like anything different from the way a man normally would behave if somebody asked him directions. We'll be behind you, but we'll keep out of sight. If we see you get out of the car, we'll come a-running. All right?"

"Check."

The two cars began to move, Madelaine Spinney and the policeman from Boston in one, Lanigan and Jennings in the other. When they reached Tarlow's Point, the woman got out and walked up to Begg's house. She rang the bell, and a moment later the door was thrown open. "Yes?"

As instructed, she raised her head from her coat collar. The two stared at each other.

"You!"

The policeman moved rapidly toward the house.

# 58

It was late in the afternoon, and Miriam watched with some concern as her husband paced the floor. Every now and then, he would pick up a book and try to read, only to put it aside and resume his pacing.

"Don't you think you ought to go over to the temple, David, just to see if everything is all right?"

"No, I'm staying home until I hear from Lanigan. Somebody will be there to check, the cantor or Brooks or maybe Mr. Wasserman."

Whenever the phone rang, he ran to it. Most of the calls were indeed for him, but he answered as briefly as possible, fearful that Lanigan might be trying to reach him. Finally, when it was almost time to go to the temple to begin the seder, Lanigan called. The rabbi listened for a moment and then smiled. "Thank you," he said, "and thank you for calling me."

"Is it all right?" Miriam asked when he hung up. "Can we go now?"

"Yes, we can go now."

The baby-sitter had been there for half an hour, waiting for them to leave so that she could turn on the TV. Miriam gave her some last-minute instructions and went out to the car. When the rabbi came out a minute later, she saw that he was carrying the tape recorder he used to dictate letters, presumably so that he could tape the proceedings. She was mildly amused at his sudden sentimentality.

When they arrived at the temple, the members were still milling around, looking for place cards, talking, trying to shift from the table they had been assigned to another where their friends were. The tables looked festive, with snowy white tablecloths and gleaming silver, and the long head table had a magnificent floral centerpiece. Drawn up to the head table were armchairs, each with a pillow to lean on in accordance with the prescribed ritual, and beside each armchair, ordinary chairs for the wives. In front of the rabbi's place were the required three matzoth covered with a napkin and the seder plate, with its egg, shank bone, bitter herbs, green herbs, and its two little dishes, one for horseradish and the other for the mixture of chopped nuts and apple.

Those at the head table were already seated, and before taking his place, the rabbi went to each one for the customary greeting and handshake.

"In good voice, Cantor?"

"Fine, Rabbi."

Mr. Wasserman looked old and frail swallowed up in the huge armchair reserved for the chairman of the Ritual Committee. He clasped the rabbi's hand with both of his.

"Always I like to have the seder in my own house, but this year my children couldn't come. And besides, sometimes for the good of everybody . . . ."

Gorfinkle had been covertly watching the rabbi's progress down the line. When he approached him, he rose and formally offered his hand.

"Stu planning to go back to school tomorrow?"

Gorfinkle shrugged. "He was hoping to, but I haven't heard from Lanigan yet. Maybe he'll call tonight."

"It's all right. He can go."

"And the others?" asked Gorfinkle eagerly.

"They too."

Emotion welled up into Gorfinkle's eyes. "That's wonderful, Rabbi, just wonderful. I don't know how we can ever thank you."

The rabbi circled the table and took his seat. He looked out across the crowded room and waited for the last person to find his seat.

When he saw that the waiters had filled all the wineglasses, he nodded to the cantor, who rose and, holding his glass high, began to chant the benediction over the wine.

The men at the head table left the room for the ritual washing of hands, and when they returned, the rabbi dipped a sprig of parsley in a dish of salt water and recited the benediction over the fruits of the earth.

He uncovered the matzoh and, removing the egg and the shank bone from the plate, passed it to Mr. Wasserman, who recited the *Holachmanya,* "Lo! this is the bread of affliction which our ancestors ate in the land of Egypt; let all those who are hungry enter and eat thereof; and all who are in need come and celebrate the Passover . . ."

Once again the wineglasses were filled, and the rabbi nodded to the principal, who was seated at one of the round tables with the family of the youngster who was to ask the Four Questions. Morton Brooks whispered to the child, who stood up and in a childish treble began to recite: *"Ma nishtana halayla hazzeh . . ."*

When the child finished, the rabbi placed on the table in front of him the tape recorder he had kept on the floor beside his chair. "The English translation was to have been given by Arlene Feldberg," he announced, "but unfortunately, Arelene came down with

413

the measles. However, we wouldn't want her to miss her portion.'' He pressed the switch — but it was his own voice that came through the machine, saying, ''Sincerely yours. Make an extra copy, will you, Miriam?'' This was followed immediately by the thin, reedy voice of the little girl: ''Wherefore is this night distinguished from all other nights?'' Weeks of coaching by the principal were reflected in the slow, stilted reading of the lines. ''All other nights we may eat either leavened or unleavened bread, but tonight only unleavened.''

The rabbi looked down at Miriam. ''You see,'' he whispered, ''I *can* bend a little.''

''And it works,'' she whispered back.

''Why may we eat only bitter herbs . . . dip our food twice . . . eat while leaning?'' Mr. Wasserman plucked at the rabbi's sleeve, and he leaned over to hear what the old man was saying. The tape recorder whirred on. ''. . . beg off from that dinner, will you, Miriam. Fib a little if you have to.'' It was the rabbi's voice.

There was a roar of laughter from the

assembled company, and Miriam hastily reached forward and shut off the machine. The rabbi blushed and said, "We will now read in unison . . ."

Dinner was served, a traditional festive meal, beginning with gefillte fish and chicken soup. As soon as it was over, a number left, pleading that their children were tired and falling asleep at the table, but most stayed on for the rest of the service with its prayers, benedictions and ceremonial songs. At last the fourth cup of wine was drunk, and the president announced, "The order of the Passover is now accomplished and prescribed according to all its laws and customs . . ." and then all called out in loud and joyous voices the traditional fervent hope expressed for centuries by Jews all over the world at the end of the Passover service: "Next year in Jerusalem."

The rabbi leaned over and whispered to Miriam, "Why not?"

"What?"

"The way things look, we'll be free next year. Why not spend it in Jerusalem?"

# 59

"You've heard the minutes of the previous meeting. Any corrections or additions? Chair recognizes Mr. Sokolow."

"Seems to me we spent most of the meeting arguing about a new contract for the rabbi, but there wasn't a word of it in the minutes."

"You left early, Harry," said Gorfinkle. "It was decided not to mention it in the minutes for obvious reasons. What if the rabbi were here today? It might be embarrassing."

"Well, so how do I know what happened?"

"I appointed a committee with Al Becker as chairman — maybe you'd like to fill him in, Al."

"Sure," Becker got up and walked to the head of the table. "We discussed mostly the terms of the contract. Some of the guys thought we ought to just make it for another five years, with a raise, of course. But there was a lot of sentiment for a lifetime contract, too. For that we'd have to discuss it with the rabbi himself.''

''So how'd you make out with the rabbi?'' asked Harry Sokolow.

''Well, we decided not to speak to him just yet,'' said Becker. ''See, something came up that I think we ought to hash out first.'' He cleared his throat. ''At the end of this year, as many around this table may not realize, the rabbi will be rounding out his sixth year with us. So the new contract will be starting the seventh year. Well, a lot of congregations give their rabbi the seventh year as a sabbatical. So we on the committee didn't want to get caught short if the rabbi raises that question without knowing beforehand the pleasure of this board. Speaking for myself, I'm all for offering it to him even before he asks.''

Immediately there was a storm of discussion.

"Plenty of temples don't give sabbaticals."

"In my brother's place they gave their rabbi a sabbatical last year, sure, but he had been there twenty years already."

"Teachers get them."

"Yeah, but only if they're going to do some special study."

"My wife tells me she heard the *rebbitzin* say they wanted to go to Israel. That seems a reasonable project for a sabbatical for a rabbi."

"What does he need it for? After all, he gets the whole summer off. I should be so lucky."

Mr. Wasserman was recognized. "The seventh year is a special time. It's like the Sabbath year. What is the Sabbath? It's something we invented, no? Six days you work, and on the seventh day you rest. Used to be people worked the whole seven days. So it's ours — an invention. And the whole world accepted it — you should take one day in the week a rest. The only one who doesn't get a rest one day in seven is the rabbi. On the Sabbath, when we get off, he works. And on the days we work he works, too. He's a scholar, our rabbi, so that every day he's at his studies. And when he's not studying, he's called different places to speak, or he goes to committees. And all the time, seven days a week, he's still got the congregation. One day a Bar Mitzvah, the next day a wedding or, God forbid, a funeral. So the only way he can have a rest is if he goes away from the congregation and the community for a while where he won't have to give sermons or be on committees or have to answer all kinds of questions. So I say, we should offer him this Sabbath if he asks for it, because I tell you the rabbi needs a rest sometimes from his congregation."

No one said anything, and then Paff muttered something in his deep bass to Doc Edelstein.

"What's that?" Gorfinkle looked up. "Did you say something, Mr. Paff?"

Paff raised his big voice and said, "All I said was that goes double — sometimes the congregation needs a rest from the rabbi."

Brennerman laughed. Edelstein chuckled.

Jacobs guffawed. Then they all laughed and kept on laughing. And Gorfinkle said, "You may have something there, Meyer. By God, I think this time you really hit the nail on the head."